# THE FALL OF
# ELIJAH GRAY

## A MOONLIGHT FALLS NOVELLA

# COLETTE RIVERA

Focus on magic
(not the hot chef)
and everything will be fine.

ISBN

Print: 978-1-99-118797-0

Kindle: 978-1-99-118798-7

# AUTHOR'S NOTE

Dear reader, if you wish to view content guidance for this book, a list of possible triggers can be found on the copyright page. This book is intended for mature audiences.

Happy reading!

# MOONLIGHT FALLS

The Fall of Elijah Gray

The Seduction of James Gray

The Cursed Sebastian Storm

The Heart of Moonlight Falls

# THE FALL OF
# ELIJAH GRAY

## A MOONLIGHT FALLS NOVELLA

## COLETTE RIVERA

# CHAPTER ONE

Elijah Gray swore he'd never move back to Moonlight Falls and refused to accept it had happened anyway. His current relocation wasn't permanent. Therefore, it didn't count.

He'd been in the small town for a week, had moved back in with his brother James, and had settled into his old room at their late grandmother's house where they'd grown up. James had been living alone in the house for years, and it hadn't changed much, making it familiar in a way Eli disliked.

Maybe if he redecorated his bedroom it wouldn't remind him how much he hated this place, like a time capsule of teen angst, sadness, and loss. But that would mean accepting he was here. Besides, it was good to remember that he'd be happy to leave no matter what happened during his stay.

Six months wasn't long, even if the dramatic part of him was convinced it might as well be forever. Eli was here to research magical anomalies in Moonlight Falls. His master's thesis super-visor thought sending him on this mission, rather than any of the other students, was perfect, almost like fate, since Eli had grown up here. Eli had wanted to argue against the sentiment, but the field research intrigued him and the project had too much potential for him to pass up.

Studying magic was his dream, and he wouldn't let his dislike for Moonlight Falls ruin it.

As much as he wished he could spend the next six months buried in books, only surfacing to conduct experiments on the vein of magical power running through town, Eli had gotten himself a part-time job at the local diner. He'd sublet his room in Los Angeles, but tuition wasn't cheap. He'd always worked alongside his studies.

He'd been lucky to find a job in a place as small as Moonlight Falls. It was a tiny blip in a sea of trees so far north in California that you were almost in Oregon. He'd worked at the town's general store in high school, but they hadn't had any current job openings. Not that he had to do more than mention to James that he needed a job. *Moonlight looked after its own*, the people here always said, and before the end of the week, Eli had been given several shifts waiting tables at the diner.

It was nice of James to look out for him. His older brother always had, even before their parents had died. But Eli wouldn't have minded if he'd had to commute to Apple Valley, their nearest neighbor almost an hour south, for a job.

Sadly, dwelling on his wish to get out of town would only make him late for his first shift.

Eli pushed his thoughts away and got out of his car, eyeing Moonlight Diner's back door. It felt silly to drive to work when the walk would have been fifteen minutes, but he'd be getting off late, and dealing with shades at night wasn't on his to-do list.

The annoying beasts could swoop around his car all they wanted as he drove home. He didn't have to worry about hitting them because their waspy bodies were made of shadows.

Moonlight Falls was notorious for its shade population, drawing tourists from all around. After growing up here, Eli wasn't fazed by the otherworldly pests, but he'd gotten used to living in a city where you could almost forget the supernatural existed. He didn't want to come face-to-face with anything from Beyond if he could help it.

Eli locked his car and entered the diner. The door creaked, announcing his arrival.

"Elijah," a deep voice called out. "That shirt looks good on you."

Eli turned to see Parker Hayes inside a small office next to the storage room. Parker assessed Eli with a familiar serious yet appreciative expression as he leaned against the edge of a desk, thick thighs taut in his jeans, long legs stretching before him. His arms were crossed over his broad chest, making the bulk of his muscles impossible to miss.

Eli felt like he'd missed the last step on his way down the stairs. "Hi."

Parker was also wearing a Moonlight Diner T-shirt. It was a snug fit, the navy-blue sleeves tight around his biceps. Eli wasn't sure why he noticed. Was it just because Parker had commented —probably jokingly—about him looking good in the same shirt? He'd known Parker for years. He was James's best friend, but Eli couldn't remember ever paying this much attention to the guy's arms.

Parker got up from the desk. "Here, I've got an apron for you." He picked up a folded navy-blue bundle and handed it over.

"Thanks." Eli unraveled it and began tying it around his waist.

"It's great to have you here." Parker clapped him on the shoulder, his grip firm and warm.

Eli fumbled the knot of his apron. He hadn't seen Parker since he'd been back. He'd skipped going over to his house with James on Sunday, even though he'd been invited. Parker looked the same as ever, square jaw lined with dark stubble, tanned skin, harsh brows, and a serious set mouth. But something was different, and Eli couldn't figure out what it was.

He shifted his weight as Parker let go of his shoulder,

searching for something to say. "I've got plenty of restaurant experience, so I'm sure I'll catch on fast."

Parker nodded. "Of course you will. I'm not worried about that. I meant it's great to have you back in town. Having you at the diner is just a bonus."

"Oh." Eli finally got the apron tied. "I mean, I'm only here for my project."

Parker frowned slightly. "Still good to have you around."

Was it? Parker had to be thinking about James. Eli couldn't see any other reason Parker would want him back in Moonlight Falls.

James was excited to have Eli home, and there was no doubt Parker cared about his friend's happiness. This would be the longest James and Eli had spent together since Eli had left for college. Normally, he only visited on holidays. He'd always seen Parker on those visits, but it wasn't like his brother's best friend had been hoping to spend more time with him.

If Parker hoped Eli was moving back here permanently, it was only in the way Eli suspected Parker hoped everyone who grew up in Moonlight Falls would return home. That was the thing about his place. The people born here couldn't seem to help coming back. Some citizens, Parker and James among them, thought the magic here drew them in.

Parker was one of the biggest believers in the mystics of Moonlight Falls. He had a strong magical ability, so maybe he was experiencing something Eli couldn't detect. As unlikely as it was, maybe Moonlight Falls really did call to people. Just not Eli.

He had no magical ability, so he was probably missing out on that magnetic pull people swore by—if it existed. Not that he minded being unable to cast spells. He could study magic academically. And there was no way he wanted to have a subconscious attachment to a place where so many bad things had happened to him.

"Why do you look like you don't believe me when I say it's

good to have you around?" Parker cocked a brow. He had more than a few inches on Eli. Combined with his bulk and stoic demeanor, it was a recipe for an intimidating figure. If Eli hadn't known Parker so well, the way he was looking down at him would have made him nervous.

Eli shifted under Parker's gaze. "I believe you. Being back is weird, that's all." Not that he was *back* back, but he didn't need to keep pressing the point.

"It wouldn't be Moonlight Falls if it wasn't weird." Parker smiled mischievously, lines crinkling around his eyes, bringing warmth to his usually cool face.

Eli swore he felt that warmth hot on his own cheeks. He laughed unsteadily. It was almost like he was nervous, but not because Parker intimidated him.

"Come on, I'll introduce you to everyone working tonight. You'll be shadowing Kaylin out front." Parker clapped him on the shoulder again, then led him out of the office and through the kitchen.

Eli's skin tingled like Parker's touch had left something electric behind. *That* had never happened before, and Eli knew they'd touched loads of times in the past. Not that he remembered any specific time. He wasn't sure why he was thinking so much about it now. People touched. It was normal.

As Eli followed Parker and listened to how the diner was run, he couldn't help thinking his reactions to Parker were anything but normal today. Eli noticed attractive men from time to time, but how could he not? It'd just been a natural observation and didn't mean anything. Eli was straight. However, he wasn't entirely sure why he had to remind himself of his straightness as Parker pointed out the staff roster with a wave of a well-toned arm.

Eli wasn't thinking about Parker's arms *like that*. He never had. He just appreciated fitness when his own body was so different, softer and paler, and probably not as strong.

He stuck his hands in his apron pockets.

"If you need anything, just ask." Parker concluded his rundown of operations. "Everyone here will be happy to help, but you can always come to me if that's more comfortable. No matter what it is, okay?"

Eli's face was hot again. It was as if Parker couldn't help looking out for him, even when he didn't need it. He'd worked in way busier restaurants than this and wasn't worried about fitting in at the diner. But he was eight years younger than Parker, and even at twenty-four, Eli suspected Parker would always see him as the kid he'd been when they'd first met.

He wasn't sure why that disappointed him.

When Eli didn't reply, Parker's attention turned assessing. "You all right? You seem different."

Eli's stomach fluttered. *Different how?* "I'm good," he insisted. "Will we be working together a lot?" He realized he'd never spent time with Parker without James. Maybe that's what was throwing him off tonight.

Parker shrugged. "Probably. The schedule can vary, but I'm here most days, even when I'm not cooking." He was the head chef and owned the diner with his parents. It had been in their family for fifty years.

"Cool." Eli nodded. Maybe he should say something more, but he couldn't think of anything that sounded natural.

Parker grabbed a white apron and slipped it on. "You're going to like it here, trust me."

Eli didn't want to like working at the diner, but he was happy he'd be seeing more of Parker and found himself agreeing. "I've always liked coming here to eat, so I'm sure you're right."

Parker chuckled. "I'm surprised you haven't asked for a piece of Moonlight pie yet."

Eli huffed. "I'm saving it for my break." The pistachio cream pie was a town classic, served with blue star-shaped sprinkles. It was Eli's favorite.

Parker's lips turned up in a sly smile. "Be good, and I'll make you a whole pie to take home one of these nights."

Eli's face went red. Parker was just teasing. That was typical of him. But the idea of being good for Parker lit Eli up like a neon sign.

He pushed the strange reaction away. It made no sense. He was being unbearably awkward tonight. Hopefully, it wouldn't be like this every time he and Parker worked together, but even if it was, at least this whole set up was temporary. The reason Eli suddenly felt weird was irrelevant. He'd be back to his life in LA soon enough, and nothing in Moonlight Falls would change that. Especially not Parker Hayes.

# CHAPTER TWO

Eli had seriously misjudged taking on the job at the diner. He hadn't prepared himself for all the conversations. Eli knew ninety percent of the patrons who came in during his first shift, and not a single one failed to comment on how great it was to see him back in town. They all seemed to take him working here as a sign he was staying in Moonlight Falls for good.

"I'm actually only here temporarily to study the vein in town," he told Tony Harris, the elementary school principal. Mr. Harris had been a teacher when Eli was younger and had spent most of his life in Moonlight Falls. A true townie if there ever was one.

"Study it?" Mr. Harris looked impressed. "Well, if that's what brought you back, great. There's lots of people here who'll have stories for you about Moonlight's magic."

Eli didn't bother pointing out that his study was based on quantitative data and anecdotes really weren't of interest. He just smiled and thanked the man before turning and taking his order to the kitchen.

"Everyone's happy to see you," Parker teased as he set a burger on the pass-through.

"Just goes to show nothing interesting ever happens here," Eli grumbled, adding the new order slip to the clips above their heads.

Parker snorted. "Come on, *uninteresting* isn't something you can accuse Moonlight Falls of. Stranger shit happens here than in LA, without a doubt."

"Then it's no wonder you like living here, you weirdo." Eli picked up the burger and turned away. He was feeling more like himself around Parker now, not so flustered.

Parker barked a laugh, calling after him, "In that case, you fit right in, Eli. Can't pretend otherwise."

Eli suppressed a smile. He'd always liked getting a laugh out of Parker. He felt light, almost fluttery, as he delivered the burger to one of James's next-door neighbors sitting alone by the window.

Other than all the chatting and the almost cult-like *welcome home* the town was giving him, the night was going smoothly. Kaylin had given him half the tables to wait on once he'd seen how she ran things out front. Tuesday nights weren't the busiest, and they probably didn't need two servers, but Kaylin said she was happy to have the help.

"You're a natural." She grinned at Eli, dimples framing her lipstick-red smile as she joined him behind the counter. Kaylin was in her early forties and had worked at the diner for as long as Eli could remember.

Eli continued rolling cutlery in napkins. "It helps that I already know the menu."

Kaylin set a new pot of coffee brewing. "Hey, we switch it up, but you're right. It doesn't change much. Some things you can't get rid of or people would riot." She laughed, and Eli smiled.

There were little signs on the tables declaring that pumpkin pie was back for the season, just as it was every September. Most people didn't need the reminder, but if the diner stopped putting out the signs, Eli had to admit even he would have asked what was going on.

The diner's décor hadn't changed in the five years Eli had been away, which he'd already known since he came here with James at least once every time he visited. The blue vinyl booths gleamed. All the pictures of the town lining the walls were the same. It made him nostalgic in a heavily melancholy way.

Eli remembered coming here with his parents and James. He'd adored the diner when he was little, coloring on the seasonal placemats they gave the kids, poking at the mini jukeboxes on the tables, and flicking sugar packets at his brother, who would send them flying back with magic. Avoiding all those memories was the other reason he wouldn't have minded commuting for a job.

After most of the tables had cleared, Kaylin sent him on his break. Eli walked through the kitchen where Parker and Aydin, the kitchen hand, were cleaning up.

"Hold on," Parker called out before he could slip past.

Eli turned. Parker held out a piece of pie on a small plate. He took it. "Thanks."

"No problem." Parker handed Eli a fork. "I was just remembering the first time your grandmother came in to buy a Moonlight pie for your birthday."

"The first time?" Eli had had the diner's signature pie on his birthday for what felt like forever, but the tradition had started after his parents died. His mom used to bake him a cake, but his grandma's talents lay elsewhere, and she'd always said it'd be cruel to subject the boys to her baking.

"Yeah." Parker chuckled at whatever he was remembering. "She said you wanted the whipped cream to be blue."

Eli's mind flooded with a scene he hadn't thought about in ages. His first birthday without his parents. James had been fifteen and he'd been turning eleven. His grandparents had gone all out to make his day special. He remembered a bouncy house and a pie that had turned everyone's tongues and teeth blue.

Eli frowned. "You were working at the diner back then?"

Parker nodded. "Full-time since graduating from high school."

Eli knew that already but hadn't thought about how it lined up with his own life. He did the math. Parker would have been nineteen then. Hell, that made him feel young. And not in a way he liked. "I'm surprised you remember. It's not like you and James were friends back then."

"No, but there's no way I'll ever forget the mess I made with that blue cream."

Eli couldn't help smiling. It had been fun, his grandparents laughing at their own stained faces in a rare moment where they were all lost in silliness together like everything would be okay. "My mouth was blue until the next day," he admitted.

Parker's eyes seemed to zero in on Eli's lips. "I really should have aimed for a baby blue, not navy." Parker blinked and looked up, his expression not matching his casual words, like he was focusing hard on something important.

"Right." Eli swallowed. His insides squirmed. "Less food coloring would have been smart."

They looked at each other for a long moment.

Eli shook himself and thanked Parker for the pie again before hurrying away. He sat in the office and looked at the pie in his hand.

It was weird thinking of Parker knowing who he was all those years ago. It couldn't be helped in a town like this, especially one with a tight-knit community that never left. Eli shouldn't care. It didn't matter that Parker had made his eleventh birthday pie.

He took a bite. The pie was as good as ever. Some people thought pistachio cream was gross, but Eli had always liked the green pudding and sweet, subtly nutty flavor. It reminded him of home in a good way and was one of the things he could admit to liking about Moonlight Falls.

The rest of the shift was quiet. Kaylin showed him how to close and couldn't seem to help telling him again how nice it would be to have him at the diner.

Eli was overwhelmed. It was hard to remain firm in the face of everyone's kindness. But their happiness at having him around didn't mean he had to like being here. The community had never been Eli's problem with Moonlight Falls, though sometimes their unwavering support had been stifling. He knew that was a ridiculous thing to complain about, but no matter what people here were like, they couldn't change the fact that everyone in Eli's life had died except for James, and he didn't want to be in a place that was littered with reminders of his loss.

At the end of the night, Eli called a quick goodbye to Parker, who was back in the office. He didn't stop on his way out the door so he wouldn't get caught up in another chat.

He stepped into the cool night air. It was only the start of fall, but after living down south, the contrast in temperatures made him shiver.

His and Parker's cars were the only ones left in the lot. Eli dug in his pocket for his keys as he made his way over to them. His phone buzzed. He pulled it out to see a message from his roommate in LA asking where the carpet cleaner was.

Eli frowned in annoyance. He'd hoped it'd be a message from a friend, saying something more substantial, but he was finding that, even after such a short time away, he was out of sight, out of mind, and if people weren't texting him to meet up, they stopped texting.

He tapped a quick reply to his roommate.

A creaking sound came from over by the cars. Eli paused, looking up. *What?* He took a few steps closer but didn't see anything. Sliding the phone back in his pocket, he unlocked the driver-side door.

Something cold wrapped around his ankle. He shouted in surprise, jumping back and losing his balance, falling hard on his backside. An inky-black hand gripped his ankle, reaching out from under his car.

It was a shade. Eli tried to scoot back. The beasts could materialize in solid form when they wanted, and the bony grip was strong. Tendrils of dark shadow wafted off its fingers, sending chills up Eli's leg.

"Fuck." Eli kicked at the hand with his other foot.

There was a hiss and the hand retreated. Before Eli could push himself up, eyes appeared, staring out from under the car. Two large reflective onyx orbs shone amidst swirling shadow.

In a sudden rush of movement, the shade lurched forward. Eli gave another involuntary shout. The beast overwhelmed him, pushing him flat on his back. It was huge. The shade's shadowy form turned solid and imposing. Eli panicked, shouting again. He had a light on his keyring but had dropped his keys and couldn't see where they'd gone.

The shade snapped its teeth in front of his face. Eli closed his eyes.

Light flared around them, bright even behind his eyelids. Eli looked in time to see a floating ball of sunlight collide with the shade's face. The beast burst into fragmented shadows and disappeared.

Parker rushed forward, kneeling beside Eli. "What happened?" He wrapped an arm around Eli's shoulders and helped him sit up.

"It g-grabbed me." Eli's voice shook with lingering shock. "Caught me off guard." It had been a long time since a shade had gotten the better of him. He felt ridiculous, but as far as he remembered, shades didn't usually make physical contact. Not unless the human started it.

Parker looked him over. "Did it scratch you?"

"No." Eli shifted out of Parker's arms. "But I'm pretty sure I'm going to have a bruise on my ass."

Parker didn't laugh like Eli had hoped. He stayed serious, worry lining his face.

Eli climbed to his feet and brushed himself off, even though he could have sat on the ground catching his breath for longer.

Parker straightened, still eyeing him. His magical display had been impressive. Calling light took a decent amount of power, and Parker had done it quickly and precisely. What was more, he didn't seem phased by the exertion. Doing magic required you to expend personal energy. In the most extreme cases, it could be deadly if you overextended yourself, but more typically, it tired people out.

Eli bent to retrieve his keys. "I dropped my light." He clicked it on and the small device produced an enhanced beam. It was a shade-light, and though it wouldn't have banished the beast back to Beyond as Parker had done, it would have scared it away.

The beam of light shook in Eli's unsteady hand. He turned it off, his heart still thumping.

"Are you sure you're okay, Eli?" Parker touched his arm, rubbing it soothingly.

"I'm fine." Eli didn't pull away this time. Parker's steady presence felt good. The shade had rattled him more than he wanted to admit. *Too much time in the city.* That had to be it.

"You look less than fine," Parker pointed out, seemingly without judgment.

Eli had to look away from him. He closed his eyes, which only directed his attention to the hand on his arm. It was an odd preoccupation, and he tried to ignore it. "Didn't that shade seem different? Bigger, or something?" He peered up at Parker. His heart pounded.

Parker's brow furrowed. "I don't think so. It seemed normal. You're just not used to them anymore."

"Maybe," he muttered, forcing himself to take a steadying breath.

"Want me to take you home?"

Eli bristled. "No, I'm good." He could take care of himself, despite recent evidence. He didn't need Parker looking after him. He was an adult, a researcher, not the little kid who needed blue whipped cream on his pie.

"All right." Parker took a step back. "And hey, don't worry about the shades. You'll be used to them again before long."

"I wasn't worried." Eli didn't bother pointing out that there was no need for him to get used to anything in Moonlight Falls.

Parker seemed to be waiting for him to leave first, so Eli got in his car. Parker didn't move to get in his own vehicle until Eli was driving out of the lot. As if he wanted to be sure Eli actually was fine to drive home.

Everything between the two of them had been weird that night. Different. Only Parker's protective side was unchanged, and it was the thing Eli wished Parker would let go of. He didn't want to be Parker's best friend's little brother. He wanted to be on equal footing if they were working together, but he also wished he didn't care. None of it mattered when he was counting down the days to leaving.

# CHAPTER THREE

The next morning, Eli woke to the smell of coffee brewing in the kitchen. He rolled out of bed and wandered down the hall to find James setting two mugs on the counter.

"Morning." His brother gave him a rare smile.

Eli rubbed his eyes. "Thanks for making coffee."

"No problem." James filled his cup. He was taller than Eli, who'd begrudgingly given up hope of outgrowing him.

The two brothers contrasted in almost every way. Eli was slim and had shaggy brown hair, while James was broad and liked his hair cropped short. James was athletic, a swimmer, and despite Eli living in perpetual sunshine, his brother was the tanned one.

James took a few satisfied sips from his mug. "I was going to make eggs if you want some?"

"Sure." Eli fixed his coffee with cream and sugar. His first sip pushed away the last of his grogginess.

"It's so much nicer cooking with you here." James cracked eggs in a bowl. "I was thinking lasagna for tonight. Haven't bothered making one in ages, but I know you'll be up for it."

"Yeah, obviously." Eli pushed away a twinge of guilt, thinking about James living here by himself. James loved lasagna, and Eli didn't like knowing James didn't feel it was worth making for himself alone.

James poured the eggs into a waiting pan. "How was the diner?"

Eli shrugged. "Fine. Quiet." He wasn't mentioning the shade. Admitting he'd been knocked on his ass was embarrassing, not to mention needing Parker's rescue wasn't something he wanted to dwell on.

James paused his egg stirring, eyeing Eli. "You didn't have a good night?"

Eli's back stiffened. "It was *fine*. It's not like I was going to love catching up with everyone in Moonlight Falls, whether I was getting paid or not."

James frowned. "I don't see why people being friendly bothers you."

Well, that made Eli feel like a jerk. "I don't mind friendly. I just don't need random people invested in my time here. Everything in this town always has to be so intense. It's too much."

James turned back to the eggs. "I'd rather be surrounded by people who care than lost in a city where no one knows me."

Eli had no doubt James would feel lost in LA or any other city. The guy had only moved as far as Apple Valley to do some community college classes and a magical electrician's apprenticeship after high school. Then he'd moved home when their grandma died so he could take care of Eli while he finished his last year of high school.

Sometimes Eli wondered what James would have done if he hadn't had to take care of him. Would he have moved somewhere else? Come to a different, more open-minded view on city living? Or would he have come back to Moonlight Falls anyway?

"There are people who care about me in LA, you know." Eli resented how defensive he sounded, especially now that he was starting to wonder how deep those friendships actually went.

"Of course there are." James popped some bread in the toaster. "Just—you don't have to work so hard at hating it here."

"I'm not." Disliking Moonlight Falls came naturally. Eli didn't understand how James could look past it all. He'd lost just as much here as Eli had.

"Okay," James relented, not entirely convincingly.

They ate their eggs in relative silence.

Eli pushed his empty plate away. He wanted to enjoy this time with his brother, not bicker. He hated the town, not James. "That was good." Eli nudged James with his elbow. "You're way better at cooking than me."

James rolled his eyes. "I'm not that talented, trust me. I hate to think what you've been eating if my eggs impressed you."

Eli snorted. "I'll spare you the details."

James shook his head, heading to the sink with his plate.

Eli grabbed it from him. "I got it."

"Thanks." James finished off the last of his coffee as Eli washed up. "I'll see you tonight then."

"Yeah, maybe we can watch a movie or something."

James's face lit up. "Sounds good." Then he was off down the hall and out the front door, heading to work at Gray Electrical, where he and Hazel Delgado looked after everything from mundane wiring to magical batteries.

Eli found magic as an energy source fascinating but not as interesting as the way magic moved naturally through the earth. Sure, it would have led to a more lucrative career if he'd gone into studying the energy production side of things, but he'd rather spend his time doing something he truly loved.

Later that morning, Eli drove into town and parked in front of the town hall. He'd officially start his project today if everything went smoothly.

The first leaves were starting to fall, fluttering in the wind as Eli climbed the steps of the whitewashed building. The town center was quaint, well-kept, and had a timelessness that made for good tourist photos. Every building had simple, classic signage, and this side of the street—with the library and the post office—looked like a small town postcard, especially when the trees were in full fall colors.

Eli approached the reception desk inside the town hall. "Hi. I'm here for a permit."

The man glanced up from his computer. "You've filled out the forms?"

Eli nodded.

"Third door on the right." He pointed down the hall.

Before leaving LA, Eli had gotten all his paperwork out of the way. His supervisor had helped secure research permissions with the state, ensuring any activity at the magical site was observational and wouldn't leave lasting effects. That left Eli to get the local permits that would allow him to set up his instruments on city council land.

"Eli!" The woman behind the desk in the small, crowded room jumped up at the sight of him. "I was thrilled to see your name when your request came through."

Eli smiled, but it felt forced. "Hi, Mrs. Gibbs."

"Please, you can call me Melinda." She came around the desk and gave him a hug. Melinda looked older than Eli remembered, but then again, he'd had no reason to see his mom's old friend when he visited. He couldn't remember the last time he'd spoken to her.

"Your project sounds fascinating." Melinda beamed at him proudly. "The best part of looking after permits is always being the first to know what's happening. I don't think we've ever had official researchers interested in Moonlight Falls. Who would have thought we'd be worth the trouble?"

"Fixed veins of power are relatively rare." Eli forgot that most people didn't think much of the vein itself. Magic was just another part of the town, like the redwoods or the shades. "The one here is especially worth looking at. From what little has been recorded, it doesn't seem to act like other fixed veins."

"Hm. Is that right?" Melinda gave him an impressed look and returned to her desk. "I'm sure you'll be able to tell us exactly why that is. Hey,"—she stopped abruptly—"do you think that's why the magic here calls to us? Because of the vein being different from others?"

"Um." Eli tried to keep his face neutral. He wasn't convinced the town "calling to people" wasn't just something people had created in their own minds. "Maybe. But I don't see how. I'm looking at anomalies in magical strength and flow. There's no evidence that strong magic draws people. Around the world, there's plenty of strong, unique magic in completely unpopulated areas."

If anything, magic repelled people. You only had to see the lack of natural magic in every major city to realize people tended to settle away from it.

"I suppose that makes sense." Melinda didn't sound entirely convinced. She turned to a pile of papers on her desk. "All I know is, something about this place feels right. My magic has never felt as soothing as is does here."

Eli collected his permits and made his way back outside, but not before Melinda promised to see him at the diner sometime soon.

He shoved the papers in his car and popped the trunk to get his instruments out. The town center happened to be the best place to begin gathering data. He knew the vein cut directly through the circular street that made up the downtown block. The diner was on the other side of the circle from the town hall, with pretty much everything else Moonlight Falls had to offer within sight of both.

Eli walked to a small, landscaped patch of grass in the center of the circular road. Flowers lined the edge in spring and summer. At this time of year, the only thing of note was the large gray stone marking the founding of Moonlight Falls that stuck out of the center of the grass. Eli placed his case next to the eight-foot stone and opened it, taking out a magical flow meter. He switched it on and walked around the area, eyes on the screen.

The vein was about as wide as the patch of grass, in this spot at least. Eli put the meter away and pulled out his recording box. He needed to study the magical energy at different points along the vein to get a complete picture of how the magic behaved. He'd start here, measuring either end of the grass patch. Then he'd move on and track how far in either direction the vein stayed fixed.

Most veins flowing through the earth moved. They didn't stay in one spot for decades like the one in Moonlight Falls had. Shifting veins had different properties than fixed ones. The changing magical flow of a shifting vein allowed this world to connect with Beyond.

Eli didn't study interactions with Beyond. He liked grounded magic and understanding how it was part of his world, so fixed veins were more his thing.

The recording box was mounted on top of a metal probe, kind of like a stake. Eli shoved it into the grass on the south end of the patch and turned the box on. He placed a cone next to it so no one would trip over it, along with a small permit sign Melinda had given him.

There wasn't much more to do before he had some data, but Eli went to his car to get his laptop. Back on the grass, he sat crossed-legged and connected the computer to the box to ensure it was all working.

A shadow passed over his laptop screen. Eli looked up to see Parker peering down at him.

"Hi." Eli experienced a pleasant jolt at the man's unexpected presence.

Parker had his hands on his hips, a sly grin stretching his lips.

"Look at that stunning smile. You must be having a good morning."

Eli looked back at his computer. "It's always a good morning when I'm learning about magic."

"With you, I'd definitely believe that." Parker squatted next to Eli. "What are you looking at?"

"Magical flow." Eli pointed to a line of numbers streaming across the screen. "Here's the amount of magical energy, and this is the rate it's moving. It's going north pretty steadily."

"Weird seeing magic in numbers." Parker scratched his chin, stubble scraping. "If you hooked this thing up to me, would you be able to measure my magic?"

"No, you need a different kind of detector for people. And not just because impaling you with the metal sensor would probably kill you."

Parker laughed. "I'll steer clear then."

Eli shut his laptop. Parker was still watching him, but Eli couldn't think of anything to say.

"I'd never have thought studying this stuff would be interesting before you." Parker tapped the box in the grass.

Eli's brows flew up in surprise. "Really?"

Parker shrugged. "Learning how to use my magic was one thing, but understanding how magic moves under the earth's surface is so abstract. It's like other galaxies and dying stars—interesting but out there."

"It's not out there. It's right under our feet."

"True." Parker stood. "So is gravity, but that doesn't mean I ever wanted to study physics. What I was saying was, that's how I saw it until you started coming home and sharing everything you learned with me and James. You're always so excited about this stuff. It's hard not to be sucked in."

"Oh." Eli busied himself with putting his laptop back in its case. Was he blushing?

"You'd be a good teacher. I could listen to you talk about veins and shifting magical patterns all day."

Eli's face was definitely hot now. "I didn't realize I rambled so much."

"You're passionate. It's not a bad thing."

Eli stood and brushed the grass off his jeans. "I guess." He wasn't used to Parker complimenting him. It had him almost as flustered as he'd been last night.

Parker gave him an expectant, almost eager look. "Are you coming to dinner this Sunday?"

"Yeah." Eli hadn't been planning on it. He was going to let James go over without him like he'd done the week before, but standing there, he found he couldn't say no to Parker.

"Great." Parker clapped him on the shoulder. "I've got to head in for the lunch shift, so I'll see you later."

Eli clutched the laptop to his chest. "Okay, see you later." He watched Parker walk away, cross the street, and disappear into Moonlight Diner.

He smiled uncontrollably the whole time.

# CHAPTER FOUR

Sᴜɴᴅᴀʏ ᴀғᴛᴇʀɴᴏᴏɴ, Eli and James arrived at Parker's house, a bowl of potato salad clutched in Eli's hands.

Parker lived in a small one-story home on the east side of town. There was a huge redwood in the back, and Parker had landscaped his front yard, turning it into a lovely garden full of native plants.

James made his way inside without knocking. "Hey, we're here," he called into the house, leading Eli down the hallway.

Eli set the potato salad on the kitchen counter as James grabbed a couple of beers out of the fridge. He popped them open and handed one to Eli. They found Parker outside, sitting with Hazel around a gas fire pit on the stone patio.

Hazel eyed them from her lawn chair. "You're late."

James grunted in exasperation. "We aren't late." He took a seat next to Hazel. She and James had been friends all their lives, since before they were born if you counted their mothers' friendship during their respective pregnancies. The only reason Parker had the title of best friend was because Hazel and James were more like twins.

Eli took the last remaining seat, which happened to be next to Parker.

"Good to see you." Parker clinked his beer against Eli's.

"Yeah, same. I mean, you too." Eli's stomach twisted. Why was everything he said so weird and unnatural? At least Parker didn't seem to notice.

It was kind of cold to be sitting outside, but looking around, Eli figured he was the only one who thought so. Hazel wore an unbuttoned flannel shirt over her T-shirt, and Parker had gone without long sleeves altogether. His arms didn't even have goose-bumps. Maybe his bulk kept him warm? Eli didn't know. James was in his typical leather jacket, but he almost never wore anything else, so having it on wasn't about the temperature.

Eli set his cold beer down, pulling his hands inside his hoodie's long sleeves to warm them.

Hazel leaned forward in her seat, resting her elbows on her knees. "I hear we have six months to convert you."

Eli looked around. "Convert me to what?"

"Accepting Moonlight Falls and moving home, obviously." Hazel took a pull from her beer.

Eli gritted his teeth. "I have to go back to LA to finish my degree."

"Of course," James agreed, shooting a glare at Hazel. "And whatever you want to do after that will be great. Wherever you want to live."

"Gee, thanks." Eli picked up his beer and took a sip. It was as bitter as the words that had just come out of his mouth.

Hazel's attention remained fixed on Eli. "Oh, come on, I thought we got over this moody phase."

He narrowed his eyes at her. "I don't know what you're talking about."

"The summer before you left, you always had that look on your face." Hazel pointed at him with her beer. "Why are you back to that?"

Eli's mouth dropped open. "I'm not."

"Lay off, Hazel," James cut in, glaring harder at her.

She shrugged. Everyone probably thought she had a point, and Eli resented it. She'd been around a lot when James moved back to take care of him. Eli had never thought of Hazel as a sister the way James did, but she was undoubtedly part of the family. Meaning, she knew way too much about Eli, including all the embarrassing teen shit he wished everyone would forget.

"Maybe we need to go for a hike next weekend." Hazel hadn't taken her eyes off Eli. "You always liked poking around the woods."

Eli had loved playing explorer as a little kid, and James and Hazel had often tagged along because he wasn't allowed to wander too far on his own. He still liked getting out in nature and couldn't deny that a hike here would be more pleasant than the dusty trails and blazing sun he'd endured in LA.

"Yeah, sure. As long as it's not raining," he agreed.

Hazel seemed pleased, leaning back with a nod.

"Are you still into spotting rare mushrooms?" Parker asked.

"What?" Eli twisted around to face him.

"A few summers ago, you were all about finding stuff in the dirt when we went hiking." Parker gestured toward the garden lining his back fence. It was also full of native plants.

"Oh, I forgot about that." Eli took another sip of his beer. He'd taken a botany class as a sophomore and gotten really into identifying plants and fungi. He'd even considered minoring in biology, but the coursework didn't overlap with magical studies at all, and it would have meant taking an extra year to earn his bachelor's.

"I learned more about mushrooms that summer than I thought possible. I still spot them sometimes, and all the facts come popping out of the depths of my mind." Parker chuckled, his attention fixed on Eli in a way that seemed fond.

Eli looked at his drink. "I can't believe you remember any of it. I hardly do." He also couldn't believe he'd talked Parker's ear off quite that badly. Parker was kind for having humored him and indulged his fixations. But then, what else could Eli expect. James was the same, and he and Parker had a lot in common.

They talked about the different trails for a while, debating where they wanted to hike next weekend. Despite always being included, Eli couldn't help feeling he was an interloper in the group. These were his brother's friends. Hanging out with them would always feel like visiting someone else's life.

He'd had his own friends growing up here, but he and his best friend, Sam, had a falling out before Eli moved away, and they hadn't spoken since. The rest of the kids he grew up with had moved away and not come back. *Yet.*

Eli wasn't sure why he added that last caveat. He didn't believe Moonlight called to people. Though if everyone else believed and acted accordingly, the result would be the same. So it made sense to wonder if his old friends would eventually return.

Parker got up from his lawn chair to start the barbecue, and James and Hazel fell into talking about work. Eli tuned them out. He was proud of his brother for reopening their grandparents' electrical shop but didn't need to weigh in on all the day-to-day drama of running a business.

Instead, he watched Parker start the coals. Heat settled low in Eli's belly. Parker was just so graceful. Everything he did appeared effortless.

Parker looked over his shoulder and caught Eli staring. He seemed to bite back a laugh. "Want another drink?"

Eli tried to ignore the fluttering in his chest. "Sure, thanks."

Parker disappeared, and Eli drained his drink. He was thinking about Parker an awful lot, and only some of that could be explained away by them working together. The weirdness from that first shift hadn't gone away, but the more Eli considered it, the more he realized whatever this was might not have started at the diner.

There had been an odd moment here, in Parker's backyard, months ago. Eli had visited Moonlight Falls for the Fourth of July before realizing he'd be back here for half the year. He and Parker had been messing around, and Eli had made a joke that sent Parker laughing so hard he'd doubled over. He'd grabbed Eli's shoulder, grip firm, steadying himself as he'd wheezed through his amusement.

Eli had been overcome with sudden nerves, almost like he had a crush on Parker. The idea had come to him out of nowhere. Eli only got that flustered around people he had it bad for, but all those people had been girls, so it'd made no sense.

He'd decided the moment hadn't meant anything. It couldn't have been a crush. Eli didn't like guys. He was just an awkward person, and that was why he'd been flustered. It was what he'd told himself, and he'd had no trouble believing it.

But if that was true, why had those odd feelings lingered, and why did everything between him and Parker seem to be changing?

Eli didn't *like* Parker. Did he?

Parker returned with two drinks and a tray of meat. Eli got up from his seat to swap out his empty beer. He paused, watching Parker adjust the coals in the growing fire.

"You seeing anyone these days, Eli?" Parker sounded casual, his focus on the barbecue.

Eli fiddled with the label on his drink. His insides fluttered and his heart rate picked up. "No."

"Thought that might be why you're so keen to get back down south." Parker shrugged.

Eli had used girlfriends as an excuse not to linger in Moonlight Falls in the past, so it was a fair assumption. "No. I haven't been seeing anyone at all." He paused. "How about you?"

"Me?" Parker turned away from the barbecue, his attention resting on Eli. "Na."

Eli drank his beer. He'd only asked to be polite. Really, there was no other reason. Still, knowing Parker wasn't seeing anyone felt…good. "It's probably not easy meeting guys all the way out here."

Parker made a noncommittal sound. "I manage." He shot Eli a conspiratorial grin.

Parker knew Eli was straight, so Eli wasn't sure what that look was about. Probably nothing to do with him, just Parker being smug about his dating prowess. Eli didn't doubt Parker did all right, looking like he did, combined with his genuine good nature. He was a catch.

"How's working at the diner going?" Hazel asked, coming up behind them.

"Good." Eli nodded. He'd only had two shifts, and neither had been busy. He hoped he'd get to work a Friday night or weekend morning sometime soon. He could handle it, and the tips would be better.

"All smooth sailing for you compared to those fancy restaurants in LA, I'm sure." Hazel raised her brows in a mockingly impressed look.

"I mean, yeah, kind of." Eli wouldn't deny it, and Hazel's ribbing was best delt with head-on. "Nothing's going to give me trouble at the diner, not compared to some of the other places I've worked." No one would be as rude as some of his city customers, that was for sure.

"Except for the shades," Parker teased as he set several steaks on the grill.

James's eyes snapped up, flicking between Parker and Eli, his posture rigid. "What shades? Did something happen?"

Eli glared at Parker, who wasn't even looking at him. "It was nothing." He turned back to face his brother. "A shade popped out at me after my first night, and I got surprised."

James's brow creased with a familiar line of worry. "You didn't tell me." He sounded hurt.

"There was nothing to tell. Really, James. It was all good." Eli hated causing his brother stress, but it was impossible not to. James had never been able to stop seeing Eli as the kid he was responsible for.

James glanced at Parker as if seeking reassurance that the incident hadn't been a big deal.

Parker gave James a steady nod. "I didn't mean it was anything major. Just a very Moonlight welcome home, reminding Eli to stay on his toes."

James seemed mollified by Parker's comment, which annoyed Eli further. Couldn't his brother take his word for it? Couldn't he be on even footing with the rest of them, or was it always going to be James, Parker, and Hazel on one level and him on another?

# CHAPTER FIVE

ELI SLEPT in on Monday morning, and by the time he woke up, the house was quiet. James would be at work, so Eli was in no hurry to get up. He lazed, enjoying the warmth of his bed, until he got bored and grabbed his laptop. He balanced it on his chest, pulling up the data from his recording box.

He sat up abruptly, and the computer slid into his lap. The live feed showed nothing, as if the vein had been snuffed out. That couldn't be right.

Making a frustrated sound, Eli opened the file showing every measurement of magical flow recorded since he'd set up the box. He generated a quick graph. Everything seemed to have been ticking along fine until two in the morning. Then it all stopped.

He shut the laptop and got dressed quickly, only pausing briefly in the kitchen to fill a to-go cup with the coffee James had left for him in the pot. Then he was out the door and driving to the town center. He parked in front of the park next to the diner and marched across the road to the grassy median.

The little cone marking his equipment had been thrown into the dormant flower beds, and the recording box ripped from the ground, left lying next to the stone.

"Come on," Eli grumbled as he picked up the cone. Wasn't one of the benefits of being in a sleepy little town not having to deal with vandalism?

Eli grabbed the recording box and immediately realized the metal probe was loose. It hadn't been snapped off, but it wasn't sitting firmly, meaning it would be useless. All the calibrations would be off and would need to be reset.

Eli swore. He'd have to contact his supervisor about a replacement or send this one south so the lab techs at the university could fix it. Week one, and he was already set back.

When doing research, you always ran the risk of having to do experiments over again, meaning if you were doing them in the field, you might have to stay longer to redo them. Eli wasn't having any of that. He'd just have to work on gathering other data in the meantime.

But what if whoever did this struck again? He couldn't continuously replace equipment. Eli turned the box over in his hands. It was powered off even though the battery shouldn't have needed to recharge for another couple of days.

He flicked the switch, and it lit up. That was good, at least. Eli turned it back off. As he did so, he noticed scratches along the sides of the box. Four distinct scrapes in the metal on either side, in a pattern like they'd been made by nails or claws.

A human couldn't have scratched metal like this, not without a tool, and that wasn't what it looked like. Most animals wouldn't even be able to do this damage. But shades could.

Had a shade attacked his experiment? But why? Eli was surprised a shade had even noticed the small instrument in the grass, especially at night. Unless the indicator light had drawn the beast in.

Shades were mischievous, and their curiosity often led to disruptive behavior. Raccoons knocked over trash cans to find food, shades did it to disrupt order. Or at least that's what people said. Still, messing up the street the night before trash day wasn't the same as property damage. Shades didn't usually go that far.

Eli gathered the cone and the permit sign and trooped back to his car. Preventing shades from striking again would be harder than if the damage had been done by a person. It's not like a video camera would dissuade a beast from Beyond.

There had been a shade at the house when he and James had gotten home last night. They'd pulled into the driveway to find the thing swooping around the front porch. Houses in Moonlight were warded, so shades couldn't get inside, and James hadn't been fazed to see the beast hanging around. He'd chased it off with his shade-light without trouble, but other worldly creatures certainly weren't something Eli would miss when he left.

THE DINER WAS busy that night. Princeton Taylor, the museum curator, ran a trivia night every second Monday, so every booth was packed. The distraction was exactly what Eli needed. And he could claim to be busy enough to escape chatting with customers for too long.

Sam was there with some other guys who worked the logging land north of town. Eli wasn't serving that table and hadn't managed to catch the guy's eye. Maybe Sam was avoiding looking at him, and if he was, that was fine. Eli wasn't sure what he'd say to his old friend anyway.

"It would be great to get an exhibit in the museum telling people about your study," Princeton said to Eli after trivia night had ended. Princeton was sitting at the counter, eating now that his responsibilities were done for the night.

"It will be a while before I have anything written up," Eli reminded him.

"That's fine." Princeton set down his tuna melt and picked up a curly fry. "It's the exact kind of local thing we should be showcasing."

The museum wasn't big. It was attached to the post office and consisted of two small rooms. Putting together a display would only be more work for Eli, but he couldn't think of a way of saying he didn't want to do it without being rude.

Maybe Princeton would forget about it after Eli left town.

That night, Parker made turkey club sandwiches for everyone working, and after Kaylin and Aydin had had their breaks, Eli joined Parker in the office to eat.

"You look beat." Parker gestured for Eli to take the chair, leaving him to lean on the desk, hovering over Eli.

"Long day." Eli tucked into his sandwich and told Parker about his ruined recording box.

"You think it was a shade?" Parker raised his brows in surprise. "That seems odd."

"Yeah. I don't know why they'd go after something so small, sitting low on the ground."

"Hm." Parker chewed thoughtfully. "Once you have it set up again, I can ward it for you."

"Really?" What a relief. "That would be great. I was going to ask James, but I wasn't sure how that would go." Eli's brother didn't have as much magic as Parker, and warding spells were draining, not to mention tricky.

"James would have just called me," Parker assured him. "Let me know when you're ready, and I'll be there."

Eli shifted in his seat. "Should I get your number then?" It was a simple, casual question, practical even, but it didn't feel that way.

"Yeah, pass me your phone." Parker set his plate down and held out his hand.

Eli passed it over, their fingers brushing.

Getting Parker's number shouldn't feel significant, but Eli had butterflies.

Parker passed the phone back. "Text me so I have yours."

"Oh. Right, yeah." Eli busied himself with sending a message. He couldn't shake seeing all his interactions with Parker through the lens of having a crush on the guy. It was like the idea had burrowed into his head and stuck. But he didn't get crushes on men. He'd never thought about kissing a guy or fantasized about things like that. He'd only ever felt that way about women.

"It'll be okay." Parker bumped Eli's leg with his in a reassuring way.

"Huh?" Eli looked up, unsure why Parker was comforting him. What was his face giving away?

"You look really concerned, Eli. I don't think I've ever seen you stare so hard at your phone. But don't worry. Once you get your box fixed, shades won't mess with it again. My wards are solid."

"I'm sure they are." Eli tried to smile convincingly. "I won't let it stress me out, promise."

Too bad he suspected he had way bigger problems than shades.

ELI LAY awake in bed that night, unable to sleep. Did he have a crush on Parker? Yes, he thought he did. Nothing else explained how he was acting.

He had a crush on a man. The idea was thrilling and panic-inducing. It felt right, familiar, but also like it had hit him out of nowhere. How could this be? Was he queer? The idea didn't feel wrong. It felt like something he'd longed for. But if it felt so right, how could he have not realized before now?

Eli didn't know what to do. He'd assumed he'd had himself figured out. He was straight. It was something he reminded himself of often.

It wasn't like he was isolated from queerness or had an upbringing that forced him to repress anything. James was bisexual, and he'd told Eli he'd liked guys in his early teen years. James had even come out publicly in high school, and their grandmother had been nothing but supportive.

So how had Eli missed this? Or had he not liked guys before now? No, somehow, his feelings didn't seem new. It was like Eli had known and not known he was attracted to men at the same time. It was confusing as hell and kind of made him want to cry in frustration.

Eli lay in the dark of his childhood bedroom and looked up at the ceiling.

He thought back to other times he'd felt inexplicably awkward around men. If he were honest with himself, the thing with Parker wasn't the first time it had happened. He'd always dismissed any weirdness, and none of the other incidents had lasted long, making them easier to ignore than Parker.

There was one college friend, Mark, who came to mind. One time, he and Eli had made plans to hang out without the rest of their group, and Eli had wondered why it felt like he was trying to ask a girl out on a date. Mark wasn't a girl, so Eli had assumed his reaction was just a flare-up of social awkwardness. He was introverted, so it made sense.

With Mark, he'd sensed he had a crush and dismissed it. But why? Lying there now, Eli couldn't understand how past him could be so dense. So what if Mark wasn't a girl. Why hadn't his mind taken the next logical step? It had felt like asking someone on a date because he'd wanted it to be a date. Had his conviction that he was straight really blinded him to any other possibility?

It was like he'd gathered evidence of his straightness and then used it to push away anything he found to the contrary. As a researcher, he knew better than to cherry-pick data to support a theory, but it had all been subconscious, and he wasn't sure why he'd started doing it in the first place.

Eli knew he looked at men. He assumed men just appreciated each other and there was more to checking someone out than what he'd been doing. More to attraction than what he'd been feeling. But that wasn't true. Eli wasn't experiencing attraction to a man for the first time with Parker. He wasn't having his first queer crush. He was realizing that his attraction to men had been there all along. Maybe it wasn't the same as his attraction to women. Maybe these crushes had been fewer and farther between, but that didn't discount them.

It should have felt good to realize all this, but Eli was overwhelmed with the sense he'd screwed up somehow. He'd cheated himself by not being honest with himself.

And what was he supposed to do now?

It wasn't like he was going to pursue something with Parker. It would never work. Parker was a Moonlight Falls man through and through. He'd never leave, and Eli would never live here. Eli liked relationships—he didn't do casual flings or one-night stands—and wouldn't consider dating someone if he couldn't see a potential future with them. There was no future with Parker.

He was the worst possible man for Eli to come to terms with having a crush on. Parker would never see Eli as more than his friend's little brother, the kid who liked blue whipped cream, the guy obsessed with mushrooms, or the city boy who couldn't handle a single shade.

But it was fine. Eli would get over his crush. Maybe he'd start dating guys in LA. He just hoped Parker didn't pick up on his feelings. He didn't need to embarrass himself on top of everything else.

# CHAPTER SIX

Eli had been on edge all week. His emotions were frayed. He couldn't concentrate. *He liked men.*

The first glimpse he had of Parker after admitting this to himself confirmed it. As Eli arrived for the lunch shift, he found Parker leaning against the back wall of the diner while talking on the phone. The big man's stance was casual, his arms bent in a way that caused him to flex, but not excessively. It was hot.

Eli wasn't appreciating Parker's build compared to his own, as some sort of ideal he hoped to be, which he'd often told himself was what he'd been doing when he'd checked out guys in the past. No, he just liked looking at Parker because he was attractive.

As Eli walked by, Parker flashed him a smile. Eli's stomach swooped.

This would be a disaster.

Eli was waiting tables with Luna that day, a woman in her thirties who'd moved to Moonlight Falls a decade ago. She was the other kind of townie, less common and more perplexing in Eli's opinion. Luna swore she'd been drawn to Moonlight Falls, first coming here as a tourist and then falling in love with the place.

"Nowhere else has ever felt like home," she explained to Eli. "I'd have loved growing up here."

Luna had a faint magical ability—as she described it—which she displayed by sweeping a few stray leaves out the front door with a spell. Moonlight Falls did seem to have a higher rate of people with magical ability in the population than was typical, and quite a few of those people seemed to stay in the town their whole lives, even if they hadn't been born here.

Maybe someone needed to study Moonlight's magnetism and see if it had any merit. But if magic drew people, why was Moonlight Falls the only place where people with these beliefs seemed to congregate? There should be cultish little magical towns all over the place.

Eli was occupied with organizing the pie display on the counter as Luna looked after their first few lunch customers. There was a single piece of cherry left, as well as pumpkin, so Eli moved them to share a stand with a partial apple pie, making room for more full pies.

He ducked back into the kitchen. "Can I grab a cherry and a pumpkin for the front?"

"Sure thing." Parker wiped his hands on his apron and headed for the fridge. It was just the two of them in the kitchen, a small radio playing on low in the corner.

"Here you go." Parker handed over two pies wrapped in cling film. Eli turned to go, but Parker caught his arm. "Hold up." He ducked back into the fridge, returning with a cake box.

Eli put the pies on the pass-through and reached for the box. "What's this?"

"Open it." Parker bit his lip like he was trying to hold back a smile.

Eli opened the lid. Inside was a fluffy pile of cream. Blue

cream. It was on top of a pie, of course, but this time it was baby blue, not navy. "You made this?" Eli asked dumbly.

"Yeah. Way less of a mess this time."

Eli huffed a laugh, but it got stuck in his chest. Why had Parker made him a pie? It gave him warm, gooey feelings, making him feel special. "Thanks, Parker." He looked up at the man.

Parker wasn't smiling. He seemed serious but affectionate. Maybe. Eli wasn't sure. "Hope this blue pie is as good as the last one."

"I'm sure it will be." Eli shifted uneasily, looking back into the cake box. Was Parker thinking about Eli as the kid he'd been back then? The reminder made their age difference seem unimaginably vast. It was a good thing Eli wasn't expecting his crush to go anywhere. "Think my mouth will turn blue this time?"

Parker shook his head. "I tasted some of the cream, and the mess was way less diabolical. You're good." Parker's gaze seemed to linger on Eli's lips.

Eli couldn't help nervously pulling his bottom lip between his teeth. "I should wait until after my shift to try it."

"Huh?" Parker looked up. "Oh yeah. Of course." He took the box back and returned it to the fridge. "I was going to give it to you later but couldn't wait, I guess."

"Um, right."

Eli knew he was being awkward. He'd reacted to the pie like it was a gift from someone who might like him back, not from his brother's best friend, who was just being nice. Had Parker noticed? Hopefully, he'd assume Eli's behavior was due to general social stumbling. Eli had never been the smoothest guy.

He hurried back out front to uncover the fresh pies and put them in the display case. He needed to replenish the coffee and roll some cutlery. There was plenty to do, and he probably wouldn't need to go back into the kitchen before his break. He needed to keep his distance from Parker. Get used to his new feelings and then get over them.

"You should come to dinner tonight," James said to Eli for at least the third time that Sunday.

Eli didn't stifle his groan. "I'm not in the mood." He tried to hide behind his laptop screen, but James continued to eye him from the other end of the couch.

"It seems like you've had a tough week." James's brows knit together in concern. "You've been quiet like you're stressing. Do you want to talk about it?"

Panic flared in Eli's chest. "Not really."

James nodded stiffly as if Eli's brush-off bothered him, but he didn't want to admit it. He frowned. "Maybe getting out of the house will help. You've been cooped up since your last shift at the diner."

Eli had backed out of the hike yesterday, claiming he had to work on background research for his thesis. "I don't want to invade your friends' lives, that's all."

James gave him a confused look, forehead wrinkling. "You're not. Parker and Hazel are your friends too. That's why they invite you to things."

Hearing that was a surprise. It felt good, like maybe James had a point and the others didn't include him because he was an obligatory extension of his brother. But he was trying to avoid Parker. Eli feared his crush would become obvious to everyone now that he'd acknowledged it. And he was afraid of his feelings growing, especially after the pie incident.

"I can stay here tonight if you want," James offered. "There's frozen pizza, and we could play a boardgame." He gave Eli a hopeful look.

Shit, the guy probably just wanted to spend time with him.

A familiar guilt settled in Eli's chest. "No, I'll come to Parker's with you. You're right. I should get out of the house. We can do pizza tomorrow." Eli wanted to make the most of his time with James and didn't want his brother to give up time with his friends just because he was being difficult.

He should talk to James. He'd understand all of Eli's confused queer feelings, but Eli wasn't ready to share. In the meantime, he had to do a better job of hiding how unsettled he was. He didn't need James worrying something major was wrong when it was just bi panic.

It wasn't the end of the world, even if Eli felt like his whole life had blown up.

James made macaroni and cheese to take over to Parker's, and Eli helped. Well, he mostly hung out in the kitchen and tried to act normal to reassure his brother he wasn't stressed while James cooked. But James seemed mollified, so Eli counted it as a win.

He didn't feel any more confident about going to Parker's by the time they left the house. Eli was officially nervous. It was as if he was going on his first-ever date, even though he'd been on plenty *and this wasn't even a date*. It wasn't anything. Parker didn't like him back. Which was a good thing. He and Parker wouldn't work together, and nothing in the world would change that.

When Eli and James arrived, Parker and Hazel were on the back patio. Everyone took the same lawn chairs as the week before, so Eli settled in next to Parker.

"Missed you on the hike," Hazel said by way of greeting. She sounded genuine, not like she was hassling him.

"Sorry." Eli gave her a strained smile. "Next time, I'll be there. I just had to focus on work this weekend." The second part was a lie, but he meant it when he said he'd join in next time. If Hazel was including him because she actually wanted to spend time with him, as James had suggested, then he didn't want to push her away.

"Sometimes work takes priority," Hazel agreed. "It's pretty cool you're studying the vein here."

Eli could admit it was cool when he allowed himself to forget why he preferred to avoid Moonlight Falls. He let the others talk, focusing on the fire. He avoided looking at Parker but didn't think he was being obvious. The flames swayed in the wind and Eli shivered.

Parker nudged his shoulder. "We can head inside if you want."

Eli was forced to look at him. "Am I the only one who's cold?"

"Yes." Hazel didn't hesitate to call him out.

"It's because we're just sitting around," Parker said in Eli's defense. "Why don't we go in and play pool or something?"

Hazel's eyes gleamed. "Great idea!"

"Not you." Parker frowned at her. "And *not* for money."

Hazel pouted. She was impossible to beat, or so Eli had heard. "Fine." She huffed. "It's a good thing I'm looking after the grill tonight, or I'd make you all pay for being sore losers."

Parker got up, shaking his head at her. He paused, looking down at Eli. "You coming?"

"Um." Eli didn't want to. Or he did want to, and that was the problem. "We can't just make Hazel cook for us while we all go inside."

"I'll stay," James offered. "Though I'll play the winner when you're done."

With no other option, Eli stood and followed Parker inside. Off the kitchen, in what might have normally been a dining room, Parker had a pool table and dart board set up. His living room was at the front of the house, along with, Eli assumed, his bedroom. He'd never been in any of the private spaces in the house, but then why would he have been? He'd never see Parker's bedroom and that was fine.

Eli picked up a pool cue. "You only wanted to play with me instead of Hazel because you think you'll win, right?"

"No, not at all." Parker grinned. "I thought you could use the practice. Really, I'm doing you a favor."

"Ouch." Eli tried to feign hurt, but he was smiling. He liked Parker teasing him.

Parker set the white ball in place. "Want to break?"

"Not really."

Parker shook his head, but not like he was annoyed. He took the shot. And yep, he looked good bent over the pool table.

Eli tried to stop checking Parker out, but it was really hard not to. Part of him wanted to lean into it now that he knew why he was looking, but this was so not the time or the guy to do it with.

None of the balls went in, so Eli took his first shot. He didn't spend much time considering which ball to aim for. He was too distracted, so, of course, he didn't get one in either.

Parker sunk his next shot, claiming stripes, but his second shot was a near miss.

"Oh, too bad," Eli teased as Parker's face fell in disappointment.

The man's lips turned up in a grin. "Still beating you."

Eli's face heated. He worried his blush would be visible and ducked his head, quickly taking his turn. His aim was so bad that he barely grazed the white ball with the tip of the cue.

Parker came around the table. "You've got to take your time aiming."

"Really? I had no idea that was how this game worked."

Parker nudged him with his elbow. "Smart ass."

Eli made a face and stuck out his tongue. What the hell was he doing? Why had he done that? It was so weird. But Parker didn't seem to mind.

Eli tried harder on his next turn, considering the table. He needed to get at least one ball in before Parker won. He found a shot he thought he could make and leaned down to line it up.

"You're aiming low."

Eli looked up from the white ball. "What?"

Parker set his cue to the side. "Here." He reached out and adjusted Eli's wrist so the cue his hand supported had a better angle.

Eli's skin prickled and he stopped breathing. Parker hadn't stepped away from him. They were still nearly touching. Eli stared at the skin on his wrist where Parker's fingers had been.

"You have to actually take the shot, Eli." Parker sounded like he was holding back amusement.

How long had Eli been frozen there? He readjusted his grip on the cue.

"See, your wrist dropped again." Parker repositioned Eli's hand, steadying the cue. He was behind Eli, bending over him so he could reach Eli's outstretched arm.

Eli's pulse sped up. The proximity of their bodies made his thoughts run wild. He liked Parker looming over him. Liked hearing his voice close to his ear. He liked the subtle touch of Parker's hand on his wrist and wished it was more.

Eli hit the white ball, and by some fluke, it hit a solid into one of the pockets.

"Nice." Parker patted his shoulder.

Eli was burning up. Suddenly, being outside in the cold didn't seem so bad. It would be better than this.

He missed his next shot.

As he watched Parker take his turn, Eli's thoughts shifted. He imagined bending over the pool table, imagined Parker's hands coming to rest on his hips rather than simply touching his wrist. He wondered what it would feel like if they were naked. If Parker touched him and pressed his hard cock against him.

Shit. Eli shouldn't have been thinking like that. The image alone had his dick perking up. He could not get an erection right now. It would be mortifying.

He told himself Parker would never be attracted to him like that, and it wasn't hard to believe. Parker had never shown any interest in him. He'd never consider Eli that way, even if he knew Eli wasn't straight.

"You okay?" Parker's voice drew Eli out of his head.

"Yeah." He rolled his eyes, thankful his arousal had died. "I just know I'm going to lose."

"Don't look so broken up about it." Parker ruffled his hair, sending chills racing all over Eli's scalp. "We can do best out of three. This is just a warm-up."

"Sure." Eli reached up and patted his hair, pushing it out of his eyes.

He had no idea how he was going to survive if Parker kept touching him. Even though the gesture was friendly, not flirty, Eli couldn't stop his body from reacting. It was like his senses were in overdrive.

They finished the game and started another. Eli put in more effort, hoping Parker wouldn't feel compelled to help him adjust his hold on the cue again.

Despite nerves making his heart race, Eli had fun. They were laughing a lot, which was good. It helped Eli cover his awkwardness.

"We should do this again," Parker said after winning his third game in a row.

Eli put his cue away. "There's always next Sunday."

"Yeah." Parker scratched his stubble-lined jaw. It seemed like he was about to say something else, but nothing came.

Eli was relieved when he and James finally said goodnight and headed out the door at the end of the evening. He needed to get home and take some me-time to sort through all the thoughts he'd been trying to ignore.

He hurried to James's truck and almost didn't notice the shade. He stopped short just in time.

The shadowy beast was hovering near the passenger door. It cocked its head at Eli and James. Before the thing could come any closer, James clicked on his shade-light and shone it in the beast's face.

The shade hissed and dodged away. James used the light to shoo it to the side of the yard. "Come on." He jerked his head, indicating Eli should get in the truck.

The shade watched them drive away, hovering near Parker's mailbox.

"That's the third one I've seen in town in barely two weeks," Eli said as they turned the corner, leaving the shade behind. "Four, if you count the one who ruined my recording box."

"Yeah, it's a fair few," James agreed, though without much concern.

Shades were more commonly found in the woods. They came into town, but Eli didn't remember it happening so regularly when he'd lived here.

They drove in silence. Eli couldn't help looking in the rearview mirrors, checking the road behind them. He swore he saw a shadow pass in front of the streetlight they'd just driven by. Another shade, or the same one following them? Both scenarios seemed unusual. Shades didn't usually seek out human contact.

At home, Eli bid James goodnight and hid in his room. Solitude felt like a relief. It wasn't that late, but he stripped off his clothes and got into bed, leaving the lights off. He lay still for several long minutes, listening to James moving around upstairs.

Pushing away the thoughts he'd had while playing pool had only been a temporary solution. He hadn't wanted to think about sex around other people, but now he was alone, and there was no reason not to.

His face heated and his dick hardened as he let the image of Parker bending him over the pool table flood his mind. *Fuck.* He really shouldn't be thinking about Parker. Eli wanted to fantasize about what it might be like to have sex with a man, but he didn't need that man to be his brother's best friend.

He imagined a generic hot guy, who maybe had a similar build to Parker, and tried to picture himself bent over a bed, but the fantasy lost some of its appeal.

Eli opened his eyes. He should just go to sleep. But he couldn't. He wasn't tired, and his cock was begging for attention.

He let out a frustrated noise, shoved the covers off his body, and pulled his boxer briefs down. He wrapped his hand around himself and gave his cock a few firm tugs.

In his mind, Parker was behind him at the pool table again, pulling his underwear down. Eli imagined the strong grip he'd felt so many times on his shoulder squeezing his ass. He let out a strained whimper, alone in his darkened bedroom.

Shit, was he really doing this? If he jerked off to this fantasy, would he be able to look Parker in the eye the next time they saw each other? Eli decided that was a future-him problem and grabbed a bottle of lube from his bedside table drawer. He could be reckless for once.

Eli returned a slick hand to his cock. He stroked himself lazily as he mentally replaced his hand with Parker's. He imagined hot breath in his ear, the scent of the cologne Parker had been wearing that night, and hot kisses pressed against his neck, trailing down his back. What would Parker's kisses taste like? How would it feel to kiss him as he jerked Eli off?

Eli stilled his hand. He was getting close already. Maybe it was because he hadn't gotten off in a while. Or maybe nothing had ever turned him on like the thought of Parker's hands on him, the bigger man's cock pressed against him.

Eli released his cock and let his fingers explore lower. He tugged on his balls before dipping his fingers between his legs. He'd fingered himself before, but this time as he traced his rim, he imagined a cock pressing against his hole. He squirmed in the sheets, trying not to whimper.

A little more lube and Eli pressed a finger inside himself. Shit, it felt good. How big would a dick feel inside him? What if it was Parker's dick?

The idea sent a jolt of lightning through him. Eli fucked himself with his finger as he imagined Parker pounding into him. He added another finger and found his prostate. Fuck, he wanted more. And he didn't want it to be just any guy filling him. He wanted the big, serious man he'd known for years. He knew Parker would take good care of him, fuck him exactly how he needed.

He massaged his prostate, wishing it was Parker's dick finding his sweet spot. Pleasure built in his body, and a couple of hard tugs on his cock later, Eli came all over his fist, moaning as his orgasm stretched out. *What kind of sounds would Parker make in bed?* Eli wanted desperately to find out.

When he finally stopped coming, Eli was breathless and sweat prickled his brow. He pulled his fingers out and lay there, blissed out, eyes closed, lube all over his hands and the sheets. It was the best orgasm he'd had in years.

# CHAPTER SEVEN

Parker poked his head out of the kitchen and into the front of the diner. "Hey, there you are, Eli. I didn't see you come in."

"Oh. Hi." Eli let his gaze rest on Parker briefly before it flitted away.

He'd purposely snuck in and hurried past the office as fast as he could when he'd arrived for the lunch shift. Last night's fantasies were indeed making it hard to face Parker. Eli had hoped—ridiculously—to somehow make it through the day without seeing the guy.

"Do you mind popping back here? I have a favor to ask." Parker held the kitchen door open expectantly.

"Sure." Eli looked at the ground as he left Luna to finish filling the salt shakers by herself.

"It's not really a favor. It's work-related," Parker explained as he led Eli to the storage room at the back. "Not exactly a normal part of a server's duties, but I was wondering if you could make a delivery for me?"

Eli stopped in the storeroom doorway. "A delivery?"

Parker turned to face him, placing a hand on a box on a nearby shelf. "Yeah, it's a long story, but the diner's agreed to deliver bulk groceries to Storm House every month. Luna's car has been giving her trouble so she asked if she could pass the task on to someone else."

Eli eyed the box next to Parker. It was full of bags of sugar, flour, and canned food. The request was almost strange enough for him to forget his embarrassment. "Why would we be delivering food to Storm House?"

The old manor north of Moonlight Falls was notorious for its creepiness. It sat isolated from the rest of the town, and no one disputed the fact that the place was haunted.

"The guy living there doesn't come into town." Parker shrugged. "He pays us well to drive out there, so you'll get a bit extra in your paycheck for your trouble."

Eli met Parker's gaze. His embarrassment was completely gone now and replaced with heavier feelings. "I haven't driven up that way in years."

"Of course." Parker ran a hand through his short hair. "Shit, Eli. I didn't think."

"It's okay." Eli crossed and uncrossed his arms, his flustered state having nothing to do with Parker for once. "It's probably not the healthiest thing for me to avoid a whole section of road just because my parents died out that way."

It had been fourteen years since his parents had died in a car crash, and Eli had been up North Road in that time. But he hadn't gone near the place since he'd left for college and didn't know what emotions driving out that way might stir up after so long.

"If you want to avoid the road, I won't tell you not to. I can find someone else to go." Parker sounded nothing but understanding.

The simple lack of judgment was more comforting than Eli had expected. He reconsidered the favor and made himself think beyond his gut reaction to North Road.

"No," he said carefully. "I think I should do it." Looking into Parker's warm brown eyes gave him a boost in confidence. "I'd rather not have it looming over me. What if I need to head up that way for my study?"

Parker nodded, his mouth set in a serious line. "You're pretty amazing, Eli. You know that, right?"

Eli's cheeks flushed. "For driving up a perfectly normal road?" He couldn't hide his skepticism.

"No. For facing things that aren't easy. For not letting things get in the way of what you want. I know being here is hard for you, but you're here anyway because nothing can dim your passion for understanding magic."

Eli was mesmerized by the look of pride on Parker's face. He hadn't realized how well Parker understood him or how much Parker had truly seen him. And from the tenderness in the big man's gaze, Eli figured Parker liked what he saw.

Eli had never expected that.

"Being here isn't so bad," he found himself saying.

"Careful." Parker smiled. "If James hears you talking like that, he'll try to get you back here after you finish your degree."

Eli rolled his eyes. But it was true. James would jump at any hint that Eli might want to come home.

Parker's serious demeanor returned. "You're sure you're good to head out to Storm House? The owner will be expecting you soon."

"Yeah, all good." Eli nodded.

Parker clapped a hand on his shoulder and squeezed. He didn't let go right away, and before Eli knew it, Parker was pulling him into a hug. Parker's embrace was warm and held him firmly, giving Eli a sense of security. He hugged back, burying his face in Parker's chest for just a second.

The physical contact sent electric tingles through his body, but not the heat of arousal. It was something deeper, making Eli forget the awkwardness brought on by last night's fantasy. The hug was pure comfort. This man understood and cared about him, and everything about that felt wonderful.

ELI DROVE OUT OF TOWN, trunk laden with boxes and a cherry pie on his passenger seat. The man living out at Storm House always ordered a pie, apparently.

It was weird that anyone lived out there, though Eli was pretty sure the house had always been occupied. The creepy property was the kind of place he and the other kids had dared each other to sneak onto when they were teens. The energy there repelled people, which Eli supposed was ideal for its reclusive owner.

As soon as Eli passed the last of Moonlight's houses, the road began to wind through the looming trees. Eli found this whole section of woods eerie, though that was his own experience clouding his judgment. There was nothing wrong with the trees. It didn't matter if it was darker up here, with less light penetrating the canopy. He only felt unsettled because he knew his parents had died out here.

But that wasn't the forest's fault. It wasn't Moonlight Falls's fault that Eli had experienced so much loss here, and in the end, driving along the road didn't upset him as much as he'd feared it would. There was a bit of sadness in his gut, but it wasn't anything he couldn't face.

Maybe he should try to deal with his loss more actively. If he could drive out here for the diner and admit it was just a place, could he see Moonlight Falls for all the good it offered rather than all the bad things it reminded him of?

He'd barely heard from his friends down south and hadn't gotten much in the way of replies when he'd asked how things were going with them. People were busy, he understood that, but being in Moonlight Falls reminded him what real community felt like. It was overwhelming but ultimately nice to be surrounded by people who cared about him and were genuinely invested in what he was doing.

The town would always remind Eli of the parents who never got to see him grow up, of his grandfather who'd died barely a year after his mom and dad, and his grandmother who'd loved him and James fiercely until she too passed away. But for the first time, Eli wanted to move on. He wanted to be comfortable with his grief instead of scared of it. Avoiding all the reminders of his loss didn't make any more sense than avoiding North Road.

Eli pulled up to Storm House. A stone wall surrounded the property, and Eli vaguely recognized the large wrought iron gate at the end of the driveway.

The gate stood open, a man leaning against it, waiting for him. Eli blinked in surprise. He'd assumed the person living here was old, assumed it was the same man who'd been living here when Eli was a kid. He'd been wrong, and what was more, he recognized the guy.

"Hello, Elijah Gray," the man called, not moving from his spot against the bars of the open gate.

"Sebastian." Eli shut his car door and stared. He'd gone to high school with Sebastian Storm, though Sebastian had been a couple of years ahead of him.

Sebastian was tall and slim, with a tumble of red curls framing his face. He sported a sly grin, his eyes narrowing as he inspected Eli. "Since when do you work at the diner?"

"It hasn't been long." Eli couldn't shake his surprise. Parker had said they did this delivery because the guy was a recluse who wouldn't come into town. But then again, Eli remembered Sebastian as a loner, and the idea that he didn't leave his property or want to socialize with anyone in town made sense.

"You have a pie for me?" Sebastian asked.

"Oh." Eli hurried around to the other side of his car to get the pie and walked it over to Sebastian. "Here."

Sebastian took it without saying thank you and opened the

lid. Eli unloaded the boxes, leaving them at the base of the driveway as Parker had instructed. He wouldn't mind carrying them to the house, except for the haunted, wrong feeling that seemed to hang over the property.

Eli was glad to avoid getting any closer. He eyed the large structure looming in the background. It was dark and unfriendly, with peeling green paint. It looked almost abandoned.

Sebastian stared at Eli silently as he unloaded the boxes, eyes drilling into him as if Sebastian was analyzing him. "So, will you be delivering my food now?"

"Yeah, I think so. For a few months anyway. I'm only staying with James temporarily. I'll be leaving Moonlight Falls in a few months."

Sebastian wrinkled his nose. "Makes sense. I don't know why anyone would want to spend time in that town."

Eli didn't know why anyone would want to spend time at Storm House. The shadows around the property seemed deeper, darker than normal. Nothing about the place was pleasant.

"You said you're living with James?"

"Hm?" Eli was startled. He'd been distracted looking at the looming trees.

Sebastian gave him a look like he thought Eli was clueless. "You mentioned your brother. Is he here temporarily too?"

"Oh yeah. I mean, no. He's got his shop: Gray Electrical. I can't imagine James ever leaving the business behind. Running it is pretty much his dream. He's here to stay."

Sebastian nodded. "Right." He didn't sound particularly interested even though he'd asked. "As great as this has been, I'm going to go." He picked up one of the boxes and turned away, not waiting for a response.

Eli got back in his car. Sebastian was kind of rude, but what else could he expect from someone hiding out in a haunted house, avoiding people?

As Eli started his car, movement caught in the corner of his vision. Eyes appeared in the shadows along the base of the stone wall. Was that a shade? Out during the day? True, the sky was gray, and with all the trees, there were plenty of shadows to draw from, but Eli had never seen one out before dark.

He drove away, leaving Storm House behind. The shades out there weren't his problem.

# CHAPTER EIGHT

ELI'S new recording box hadn't arrived yet, but he had to map out the vein's location and measure the power running through it. With that in mind, he was back in the town center with his handheld magical flow meter.

The placement of the vein in this part of Moonlight Falls was inconvenient. Other than the patch of grass the town circle was centered around, the vein ran through the street. It wasn't wide enough to make it to the sidewalks on either side, but Eli wasn't letting that get in his way. He'd borrowed a bright-orange safety vest from James and was carefully wandering the road.

Moonlight Falls didn't have a lot of traffic, and he'd been standing in the middle of the street on the south end of the circle for a good five minutes before anything disrupted him.

"Eli," a familiar voice called.

He smiled, looking up from the flow meter. "Hi, Parker."

"What are you doing?" Parker's lips twitched in a bemused grin.

Eli pulled a map out of his pocket. "Mapping the vein. It goes right through the center of Main Street." He pointed down the road toward the south end of town.

"You can't just walk around in the middle of the street with your eyes glued to that screen."

Eli huffed. "I'm being careful. Besides, how else am I supposed to follow the vein?"

"Why don't I drive you?" Parker crossed his arms. "That way, you can look at your screen and map, and no one will run you over."

"That's actually a good idea," he admitted.

"I'm free all afternoon. I'll go get my car." Parker grabbed Eli's hand and pulled, guiding him out of the street and onto the sidewalk. "Wait here."

Eli's heart fluttered as he watched Parker head over to the diner parking lot. Maybe he should feel silly because Parker acted like he needed looking after, but the offer to help only warmed him.

A minute later, Parker pulled up next to Eli and he climbed in the car. "So where to?"

Eli laid his map on his lap and took a pen from his vest pocket. "Straight down Main Street, but go slow. I've got to give the meter time to get a reading and don't want to miss the vein veering off in another direction."

"You got it." Parker pulled away from the curb.

Eli watched the meter screen with keen attention, glancing up every once in a while to check where they were. They made it all the way down the block, past the B&B and the elementary school. The vein stayed as straight as the road.

After another block, Eli called out, "Stop."

Parker pulled over. "What's up?"

"It disappeared." Eli put a dot on his map. "I should get out and check what's going on."

Parker climbed out with him. They were at the start of the southern neighborhood. After checking the coast was clear, Eli walked into the middle of the road, heading back the way they'd come until he found the vein again. Parker seemed happy to supervise from the sidelines, and Eli tried not to let Parker's attention become a distraction.

He walked around until he found the point where the vein and the road stopped aligning. Main Street curved off to the west. The vein, however, left the street and headed straight over the sidewalk and through someone's private property. Eli spread his map on the hood of Parker's car and drew the line.

Parker peered over his shoulder. "Does the shape mean anything?"

"Hm, not necessarily." Eli glanced up at Parker and was struck by the focus in his gaze. Focus on Eli, not the map. "Straight formations are rare, but it may or may not have anything to do with the power moving through the vein."

Parker nodded, thoughtfully absorbing the information. "So where to next?"

"I can't exactly follow it onto people's property without permission. Let's go check out the north side of town and see if we can track it going that way, through public land. I'll come back here later and knock on doors."

"Righty-o." Parker climbed back in the car. He was such a good sport for putting up with this.

The side of the vein cutting through the north half of the town circle was just as straight as the southern end. Parker drove them slowly up Main Street, following the vein past Gray Electrical, the thrift shop, and the few houses out this way. They continued along North Road, which didn't start winding until you left town.

The road turned, heading into the trees toward Storm House and the logging lands beyond. At Eli's request, Parker pulled over, and the two of them got out. Eli used his meter and followed the vein off the road and onto the shoulder. It seemed to keep going straight, but a creek stopped him from following it farther.

"Wonder where it goes." He looked off into the trees.

"I can tell you're itching to wander," Parker said from beside him.

"It's tempting, but we've made good progress today."

Parker bumped his shoulder against Eli's. "Sounds like we deserve a treat then."

"Oh?" Eli smiled, buzzing from the small contact between them.

"Yeah, I think I might need an ice cream." Parker acted like it was serious business, making Eli laugh.

They drove back to the town center and stopped in the ice cream shop next to the B&B. Eli got a chocolate waffle cone and Parker ordered a scoop of the "spooky" ice cream.

"I cannot believe you got that." Eli shook his head at what was essentially cookies and cream with ghost marshmallows and bat-shaped sprinkles on top.

"But the ghosts are so cute." Parker picked one up with his spoon. "Let me have my fun."

Impulsively, Eli flung his arm around Parker. "I'd never deny you."

Parker laughed, a low, full-bodied rumble. Eli felt himself flush. He pulled his arm away. Was Eli flirting? It certainly seemed like his crush had evolved beyond the awkward stage and settled somewhere more confident. And Parker was... Was he flirting back? He was grinning at Eli with this soft look in his eyes.

No, Parker wasn't flirting. He was just being nice. Just keeping Eli company and making sure he didn't get run over. Looking out for him the way James did. Parker cared, but that didn't mean he'd ever be attracted to Eli.

They ate their ice creams. Eli tried not to watch Parker lick his spoon. The man had full lips that would no doubt taste sugary sweet right now.

"That was good." Parker threw his cup in a nearby trash can. He turned to face Eli. "Want to hang out again sometime?"

Eli was confused. They hung out all the time, didn't they? "Yeah, sure." He bit off a piece of his waffle cone.

"We can do some more mapping together. Maybe head out into the forest along one of the trails." Parker ran a hand through his hair. "Or maybe we could just watch a movie. That one you told Luna and me about the other day sounded funny."

"Yeah." Eli stuffed the last of his cone in his mouth, trying to ignore the butterflies in his chest. There was no need to get carried away. Parker was just being nice.

# CHAPTER NINE

Eli wasn't sure when it had happened, but he was wholeheartedly enjoying working at the diner. He'd stopped trying to escape conversations with customers and even found himself getting sucked into stories about people's personal feelings on the magic here. There was so much love for Moonlight Falls, and Eli had to admit he got it. This place was special, even if it was a bit odd with the shades and places like Storm House.

Eli understood why people liked it here, and while sometimes the familiarity made him melancholy, there was a lot of comfort to be had in Moonlight Falls. He certainly wasn't an outsider. He wasn't really a city boy, no matter how long he'd lived in LA.

He overheard some tourists discussing how creepy they found the town as he delivered their meals. They said the magic felt foreboding, but it was exactly what they'd expected, coming here on a supernatural tour looking for a thrill.

Moonlight Falls wasn't creepy. Eli shook his head at the ridiculousness.

"You up for a movie after work?" Parker asked as Eli brought some dirty dishes into the kitchen.

"Yeah, why not." They'd probably be getting out of there on

the early side that night, so there was no reason they couldn't hang out.

Still, when the time came to leave, Eli experienced a flutter of nerves. He wanted movie night with Parker to be more than just two friends hanging out. He wanted to see if his crush could ever be more, wanted to find out if there was a chance his feelings weren't one-sided.

But he was scared. He worried Parker would never see him like that, that they'd met when Eli was too young for him to ever be a potential romantic partner in Parker's eyes. But Eli was less worried about there being no future for them if Parker shared his feelings. Maybe there could be. Not hating Moonlight Falls and holding on to every bad memory felt good. A relief Eli hadn't known he'd needed.

Eli might not be as in love with this town as some of its citizens, but there were worse places to live. There was plenty he didn't like about LA and a lot he wasn't looking forward to returning to.

For the first time in Eli's life, it felt like there was potential in this small town.

He shook his head as he got in his car. Was he really getting sucked into Moonlight Falls? The one thing he swore he'd never do. Or was he just falling for Parker Hayes and, by extension, Moonlight Falls, unable to help seeing the good in the place Parker loved and devoted his life to?

Maybe it was Moonlight's magic drawing him in at long last. Eli laughed at himself for even having the thought.

He shot off a text to James, letting his brother know he was hanging out with Parker after work. James would worry if Eli didn't come home, and even though sending word made Eli feel like a kid staying out late, it was worth it to know James wasn't working himself up, thinking something had happened to him.

A shade followed Eli as he drove to Parker's. It stayed back as he got out of his car but seemed to watch him. He'd seen the beasts more nights than not and was almost getting used to them. At least none of them had tried to grab him since that first night.

"Mind if I take a quick shower?" Parker asked as they got inside. Parker had driven his own car home, and Eli had followed. "I smell like the diner."

"No problem." Eli glanced around Parker's entryway. It looked the same, but being here felt different without James. "I usually shower after work too."

Parker hung his jacket up on a hook by his front door. "There's a shower in the guest bathroom if you want one."

Eli took his own jacket off. "Eh, my clothes probably smell like fries, so what's the point?"

"I can lend you something."

Eli paused. The idea of wearing Parker's clothes was appealing. "Okay, thanks."

Parker disappeared into his bedroom, returning with a folded pair of joggers and a T-shirt. "Knock yourself out."

Eli shut the door to the hall bathroom. Showering after a restaurant shift always felt like heaven. Even being in an unfamiliar place didn't detract from Eli's relaxation. He sniffed the shampoo sitting on the edge of the tub. It smelled like Parker.

The clothes were too big, but Eli didn't mind. He didn't really care how he looked. He was doubtful Parker would ever look at him that way, no matter what he wore. But that didn't mean he couldn't enjoy tonight. He liked being here with just the two of them.

Eli found Parker in the living room, sitting on the couch.

Parker's eyes swept over him, probably noting how badly the borrowed outfit suited his smaller body type. But Parker smiled. "I've never seen you look so cozy."

Eli's cheeks flushed. He had no idea how to respond, so he didn't. He just made his way over to the couch.

Parker sat in the middle, meaning wherever Eli sat, they'd be close together. Parker must have thought nothing of it, but Eli was feeling nervous. He didn't know what he was supposed to be doing or even what he wanted to be doing. He needed his crush to be a secret but was also dying for more.

He plopped down to the left of Parker.

"Can I pick the movie?" Eli tried not to stare at Parker's wet hair or breathe too deeply now that Parker smelled fresh and inviting.

Parker held out the remote. Eli reached for it, but Parker snatched it back. "I don't know. I was kind of hoping to pick. Unless you really want to."

"I do." Eli snatched at the remote, but Parker kept it out of reach. He laughed. "Why are you being like this?"

Parker dangled the remote above Eli's head, a mischievous grin pulling at those full lips. "Like what?"

Eli pounced, grabbing the remote and falling onto Parker in the process. Parker didn't give in. He grabbed Eli around the middle and dug his fingers in, tickling him. Eli shrieked and squirmed but didn't let go of the remote. He flopped back onto the couch, trying to get away. Parker followed him down, pinning him to the cushions with his firm body.

Eli gasped as Parker's weight came down on him. Parker grabbed for the remote. Eli wasn't so dumbstruck that he was going to give up. He attempted to push Parker off, but Parker caught his wrists and pinned them above his head.

Eli struggled, no longer caring about the remote clutched loosely in his hand. "Parker." He meant to laugh or sound annoyed, but his voice was breathless. He felt so good with Parker on top of him.

Their eyes met, and Parker held his stare. A devilish grin lit the man's face. "You going to give it up?"

Eli's body flushed with heat. He struggled again, but not really. Not because of the remote or to get Parker off him. He wanted Parker to pin him down tighter, to feel him more. He didn't ever want to leave Parker's hold.

Parker encircled Eli's wrists with a single, large hand, freeing his other. Eli's breath stuttered as Parker plucked the remote from his grasp.

"Got it," he teased, smug and smiling.

Eli's pulse pounded. His body sang. It felt amazing to be pinned like this. By a man. By Parker. Eli wanted more. He wanted this, but with both of them naked. Unable to keep the arousing thought at bay, his dick hardened.

Parker's thigh was pressed tight between Eli's spread legs, so there was no way he'd missed Eli's erection. Parker was still looking into his eyes, all silliness replaced with something that looked like longing.

"Parker?" Eli whimpered, squirming half in embarrassment, half in need.

Parker dropped the remote, his other hand slacking on Eli's wrists but not letting go. "Yes, Eli?" His voice was husky, serious, his attention clearly focused as he searched Eli's face.

"What if—um—I wanted—" Eli sucked in a breath. His gaze locked on Parker's lips. He was terrified, but his desire outshone everything. "What if I kissed you? Would you want—I mean— would you like…?" His words failed and his face burned. He couldn't think straight, and for a second, he was filled with fear of rejection. His clumsy words wouldn't capture a man like Parker's desire.

Parker ran a hand through Eli's damp hair. "Yes, I'd like to kiss you very much, Eli." He moved his other hand off Eli's wrists, letting it rest by his head.

"Oh." Eli's heart soared. Parker wanted to kiss him. *Oh god,* Parker wanted to kiss *him.*

Before Eli could second guess anything, his hands were in Parker's hair. He pulled Parker down to meet him, and their lips brushed. Eli kissed Parker carefully, savoring it and letting Parker's intoxicating scent overwhelm him.

Parker kissed back, matching Eli's gentle movements. His lips were as soft as Eli had imagined, but it was like no other kiss he'd ever had. Every scrape of stubble against his cheeks was a beautiful reminder of who he was kissing.

Eli groaned. At the sound, Parker leaned in and deepened the kiss. Eli opened for him, moaning once more when Parker's tongue entered his mouth.

His pulse pounded and his cock ached. The kiss felt like a jolt of electricity. A shock that reset his whole world and pulled things he hadn't even realized were blurry into focus.

Eli squirmed under Parker, and the bigger man smiled against his mouth. Parker rolled his hips, and Eli felt a growing hardness against his hip. Parker was hard for him. *For him.* The knowledge made Eli dizzy.

They kissed like they'd both been waiting years for this moment. Parker's hands ran up and down Eli's arms and over his shoulders, cupping his upper back. Then he pulled Eli up and over him as he lay back, switching their positions.

Eli yelped in surprise. He'd never had someone pick him up in an intimate situation, but apparently, he liked being manhandled.

Eli spread his legs wide in the new position, straddling Parker's lap. Their erections pressed together, only separated by the soft cloth of their joggers. Parker hummed into Eli's mouth as Eli settled into place. His hands moved from Eli's shoulders down his back, sending tantalizing chills across Eli's spine.

It felt so good. Everywhere Parker's hands went was like a spot no one had ever touched. Somehow, their physical contact felt new, foreign, and exciting, but right, like coming home.

Parker's hands slid lower until they cupped Eli's ass. Eli moaned as Parker took a firm hold of him, big hands spread wide. Parker pulled Eli close, guiding Eli's hips into a rolling motion as he palmed Eli's ass. Eli rubbed against Parker enthusiastically, and Parker squeezed him tighter, kissing him harder.

Eli's whole body was on fire. He cried out as the intense release of his pleasure came out of nowhere. An orgasm overwhelmed him, his whole body stiffening as he came from the feeling of Parker's hands on his ass and their cocks so close together.

Eli broke their kiss, panting, and laid his head on Parker's chest. Parker's hands remained on Eli, his dick still hard between them.

Eli froze. *Oh god.* How had that just happened? What had just happened? He'd never come like that before, with no warning. And it was so obvious he'd had an orgasm, from the way he'd moaned to the uncomfortable wetness in his underwear that was bound to seep through his joggers for Parker to feel. They'd only been kissing. Eli wasn't supposed to get off from that alone.

He was panicking. He didn't know what to do now and couldn't seem to move.

"What's going through that busy mind of yours, hm, Eli?" Parker's words were soft as his hand stroked Eli's hair.

"I wasn't expecting—um—*that*," Eli whispered. "Sorry. I—I think I'm just overwhelmed."

"No need to be sorry." Parker continued stroking his hair. "We sure went from zero to a hundred."

Eli smiled and tucked his face into the crook of Parker's neck, his panic abating. "I've never kissed a man before." The whispered words felt safe with Parker. He made Eli feel like he had nothing to worry about. "I've wanted to kiss you so badly." He closed his eyes for a second. "I didn't think quite that badly though."

"I've been dying to kiss you too, Eli."

Eli stopped hiding his face. He pulled back and looked down at Parker. "You have? But you thought I was straight."

Parker bit his lip like he did when holding back a smile. "Did I? We haven't ever talked about your sexuality, but I've got to say, the way you've been checking me out has been far from straight behavior."

"Oh." Eli felt lost again. He'd been totally obvious.

Parker brushed back a stray lock of Eli's hair. "I've been feeling something growing between us for a while now. At least on my end. The last couple of times you visited."

"Really?" Eli's head was swimming. Had he missed this too? Was he totally clueless? Or had he just not picked up on Parker's feelings because of the same assumptions that had caused him to misread his own?

"Yes, really." Parker's cheeks darkened in a blush.

Did that mean Parker didn't think he was too young? Had Parker been trying to take care of Eli not because he saw him as the kid he used to be but because he'd wanted to express his feelings—romantic feelings—for Eli?

Eli leaned in and kissed Parker. This was wild. He was so happy. They were kissing and talking, and Eli had never felt so close and comfortable with someone—with drying cum in his pants, to boot. He let out a slightly hysterical laugh.

Parker cupped his cheek. "You all right?"

"Yeah." It was Eli's turn to blush. "I might go, um, clean up."

Parker's grin turned mischievous. "Good idea." Then he pulled Eli close so his lips brushed Eli's ear. "That was one hot fucking kiss."

Eli's breath caught. "Glad you thought so."

He extricated himself from the couch and went to the bathroom, feeling like he was floating on a cloud.

Him and Parker!

# CHAPTER TEN

ELI RETURNED to the couch and tucked under Parker's outstretched arm. They put on a movie, but Eli didn't watch a second of it. His whole attention was on the man holding him.

He slid an arm around Parker's waist and let his head rest on Parker's firm chest. Parker ran his fingers through Eli's hair. Cuddling had never felt so good. Eli wanted to touch Parker everywhere. His heart pounded throughout the whole movie. That feeling of everything being new but so right hadn't gone anywhere.

They didn't kiss again, and Eli was fine with that. Snuggling was thrilling enough, but as the movie ended, his doubts set in. Did it mean anything that they hadn't kissed more? Had Parker changed his mind?

Eli should've offered to return the favor and gotten Parker off, but earlier, everything had felt so natural and perfect just how it was. It hadn't crossed his mind. He wasn't sure he was ready for more right this second.

Eli felt his inexperience acutely. He'd admitted that he'd never kissed a man and knew Parker wouldn't judge, but what if that fact made Eli less appealing in Parker's eyes. It seemed like Parker had guessed Eli's queerness and hadn't known Eli was walking around thinking he was straight. Maybe Parker assumed Eli had been with men before. What if hearing Eli had no idea what he was doing had given him pause?

Parker kissed the top of Eli's head. "This was fun. We should do it again sometime."

Eli tightened his arm around Parker. He shouldn't be worrying so much. It was just his insecurity talking. Parker sounded perfectly happy. Eli had to give the guy some credit. Parker didn't seem like the kind of person to get hung up on Eli's inexperience, and knowing Parker, he'd tell Eli if something bothered him.

"Yeah, I'd like that." Eli reluctantly extracted his arm from around Parker and pulled back. "I should head home."

Parker walked Eli to the front door. He grabbed his dirty clothes from the bathroom and pulled on his jacket. His cheeks were red as he said goodbye, nerves churning in his belly.

As distracted as he was, Eli didn't see the shade until it hissed at him. He stopped short. The beast hovered next to his car, its smirking, pointy teeth protruding past its lips. The way it was focusing on Eli had him worried it was about to pounce. He shoved his hand in his pocket, digging for his keys.

The shade drifted closer. Eli pulled out his shade-light and flicked it on. The shade dodged the beam but didn't retreat. Eli shone the light in its face, causing it to hiss again as it darted upward.

Eli quickly made his way to the car. The shade grabbed him from behind, yanking on his jacket. Eli whirled around, trying to point the light, but the shade didn't let go. Eli willed himself not to panic. The last thing he needed was to scream and have Parker come rushing out. He didn't want Parker to see him as someone who needed to be protected. He wanted to be on even footing more than ever, and needing rescuing wasn't going to help achieve that.

He yanked his jacket from the shade's grip and shone the light in its eyes. As the shade darted away, Eli followed it with the light beam, forcing it farther away. Then he quickly darted to his car and jumped in.

With a bang, the shade was at his window, hitting it with its fists. Eli gasped in surprise. Why was this one so aggressive? He started the car and pulled away, but the beast followed him all the way home.

Eli parked in the driveway of James's house. He had to shine his light out his window to push the shade back just to get out of the car.

He ran to the front door and threw it open. Once he was inside the wards, the shade couldn't get him. It hovered just beyond the threshold. Eli shone the light in its face one last time. It hissed and shot out of the way, retreating toward the car.

Eli closed the front door, suddenly exhausted. Shades were never this aggressive. Eli knew he wasn't just misremembering his childhood or too used to city living. This was weird, even for Moonlight Falls. But if something was going on, if the shades around here were changing their behavior, surely other people in town would have noticed.

Maybe the shade tonight was a fluke. Though Eli couldn't help feeling like he was being targeted. Almost like the shades, or one shade in particular, had been stalking him since that first night. But that wasn't how shades behaved. They didn't stick around. They usually just passed through Moonlight Falls before disappearing into the woods.

Eli couldn't shake the feeling that this shade was the same one that had grabbed him from under his car. No one would believe him if he voiced this fear. He'd only be told that all shades looked alike, and he was mistaken. And they did all look similar, like any other wild animal. You probably couldn't say if the two random deer you saw briefly running through the woods were actually the same.

Besides, Parker had banished that first shade back to Beyond. It wouldn't come back for him. That was ridiculous.

Eli pushed the thoughts away. He resolved to buy a more powerful light and went to bed.

THE NEXT NIGHT, James seemed tired when he got home from work, so Eli offered to make dinner. He hadn't been lying about not being a good cook, so he stuck with sandwiches, and James seemed happy enough.

"How's your research going?" James asked as they settled on the stools at the kitchen counter, plates in front of them.

"Good. I got my recording box back today." Eli was going to text Parker tomorrow about warding it and was pretending he wasn't nervous about it. Everything to do with Parker made his insides flutter.

James didn't dig into his sandwich right away. He seemed too focused on Eli. "Are you worried about your project?"

Eli put his sandwich down without taking a bite. "No." He paused, both wanting and not wanting to talk to James about what had really been on his mind.

"I'm sure everything else will go smoothly," James offered, clearly trying to soothe what he thought were Eli's worries about his research.

"Yeah." Eli tucked into his food. By the time he'd finished the first half of his sandwich, he'd convinced himself to go for it. "How did you know you were bi?"

James's eyebrows raised in surprise, but only briefly. "My first crush on a guy got me thinking, I guess."

"Right." Eli was disappointed by the simplicity of the answer, even though he tried not to be.

"I don't know," James went on with a shrug. "It wasn't

just that. But I guess I had feelings for guys before I ever felt that way about girls, so I spent a decent amount of time trying to figure out if I was gay. But by the time I was in high school, I was pretty confident I liked people of any gender."

Eli nodded. Why had he ignored some of his crushes? James didn't seem to have ever had that problem. Maybe Eli shouldn't be looking for answers in James's experience—it wasn't the same as his—but he couldn't help it.

He wanted to tell James he thought he might be bi but wasn't sure how. It felt so awkward to blurt it out. He wished he didn't have to. He wished people wouldn't assume he was straight just because he'd only ever dated women. Yes, he'd made that same assumption himself, but how could he not have fallen into thinking like that when being surrounded by that assumption his whole life was a big part of what had made it hard to see himself clearly?

It was messy and frustrating, but maybe James didn't think Eli was straight. Parker hadn't.

Eli ate the rest of his sandwich. "I think I've only just figured it out," he said when his plate was empty.

James shifted in his seat to face Eli. "Figured what out?"

"That I'm queer, or bi, or something." Eli shrugged helplessly, letting his arms flop.

James smiled. "That's awesome." He got off his stool and hugged Eli.

Eli's chest pinched as he hugged his brother back. "Yeah." He smiled.

James released him. "Thank you for sharing with me."

Eli rolled his eyes, overcome with affection for his brother and needing to counter it. "Of course I'd tell you." He paused. "Did you know?"

"Know you were queer?" James considered. "No. I mean, I'm not totally surprised, but it's not like I'm sitting here thinking I've always known." Their grandmother had said something along those lines when James had come out.

"That's good." Eli rubbed the back of his neck for something to do with his hands. "I'm glad I wasn't the only one oblivious while everyone else knew."

James gave him a funny look. "Figuring yourself out now doesn't mean you were oblivious before."

"But I kind of think I was. All this stuff was there before now, and I didn't realize what it meant."

James squeezed his shoulder. "The important thing is you know yourself better now, and that's nothing but a good thing."

Some of Eli's conflicted feelings eased. James was right. He should cut himself some slack and not worry so much about his past or how long it'd taken him to sort out his feelings. He didn't have to feel bad about this happening now versus sooner. Eli knew people came out to themselves at any age, and really, he was still pretty young in the grand scheme of things.

He could wish he'd figured it out sooner or that he'd never bought into the assumptions that made him dismiss his own emotions, thinking what he'd experienced wasn't "queer enough," but he shouldn't beat himself up about it.

"I'm glad I told you." Eli smiled. "Now you can stop worrying about me being stressed. I was just freaking out about this, but I'll be fine."

James laughed. "I wasn't worrying."

*Yeah, right.* Eli patted his brother's shoulder. "Sure you weren't."

James gave him a sheepish look before collecting their plates. "I'm glad it's nothing else."

Eli thought of Parker, but there was no way in hell he was bringing *that* up.

Parker met Eli in town the next afternoon to put a ward on his recording box.

Eli got butterflies as soon as he caught sight of Parker crossing the street toward him. "Hi."

"Hey, gorgeous." Parker grinned at what must have been a look of shock on Eli's face.

No one had ever called him gorgeous before. He really liked it.

Eli had no idea what was going on between them. Would they start dating? Did Parker want that, or did he just like flirting now that they'd acknowledged their mutual attraction? Either way, Eli couldn't mess this up. Parker would always be in his life via James. He couldn't let anything that happened between them ruin the friendship they had or make things awkward. If Eli was going to try and figure out *something* with Parker, he had to do it right. Eli had to figure out what he wanted and go in knowing what he was aiming for.

If Parker was up for something serious, a relationship, and not just a few kisses and flirty words, then Eli had to be prepared for what that meant: Moonlight Falls. Could he see a future here beyond the next six months? Admitting to liking the town wasn't the same as considering staying.

But looking around the town center, he didn't completely hate the idea.

"You should be good to go." Parker straightened, getting off the ground after completing the warding spell on the recording box.

Eli had set it up in the same spot as before. "I really appreciate it. Could you give me a copy of the spell? I need to put it in the methods section of my thesis."

"Yeah, no problem." Parker tucked his hands in his jacket pockets.

"Can I get you an ice cream as a thank you?" Eli's stomach flipped like he was asking Parker out on a date.

Parker grinned down at him. "Of course you can."

Eli got two scoops of the "spooky" ice cream and handed one to Parker.

Parker gestured to the cup in Eli's hand. "I see you've been converted."

Eli groaned. "Oh my god, you sound like Hazel."

"Sorry." Parker laughed.

They made their way across the street to the park just as a group exited the diner next door. Eli found himself face-to-face with Sam. His old friend stopped and stared like he'd been frozen.

"Hi." Eli waved.

Sam broke eye contact before looking reluctantly back at Eli. The other guys he was with stopped halfway down the block, waiting. "Hey, Eli. Surprised to see you back here."

"Yeah." Eli made an awkward motion with his arms, like a flailing shrug. "Look, Sam, I'm sorry about the way I was before I left."

The tension seemed to leak out of Sam. He ran a hand through his messy black hair. "That's okay. I get it. I mean, I didn't at the time, but I get now that you weren't mad at me. You were mad at this place and everything that happened here."

Eli cringed. "Yeah, I wasn't in a good place at the end of high school, but I didn't have to take it out on you. I was such an ass, acting like I was better than everyone for leaving." He hated thinking about how rude he'd been to Sam the last time he'd seen him, basically shitting on him for wanting to stay in Moonlight Falls.

"If I were you, I would have left too," Sam said with more understanding than Eli deserved.

"Well, now I'm back, so you can have the last laugh."

Sam smiled. "You're sticking around? I thought you were doing some project."

"I'm not sure. Maybe I'll stay," Eli admitted. Parker had drifted over to a bench in the park, away from the conversation. Eli felt it was fitting that Sam was the first person he told he might want to stay here. "I was wrong for hating this place so much."

"That right?" Sam shook his head. He glanced over at his friends. "I've got to run. We're only on our lunch break. But hey—if you want to join us for trivia the next time you're not working, let me know."

"Okay, thanks." Eli was dazed as he walked over to Parker. He was relieved he'd been able to talk to Sam. He'd felt guilty about the end of their friendship for years but had mainly tried to ignore it.

They might never be best friends again, but knowing Sam understood and didn't hate him was a relief Eli hadn't thought he'd get. It was just another thing about Moonlight Falls that was shifting before his eyes, another bad memory that had become more comfortable.

Being stuck here and confronting the past, rather than visiting for a few days only to run away, had been good for Eli. He only wished he'd done it sooner.

# CHAPTER ELEVEN

HALF A WEEK LATER, both Eli and Parker had the night off. Parker had asked, very casually, if Eli wanted to hang out. Of course Eli had agreed, and he was driving over to Parker's house full of excited nerves.

It wasn't a date. Neither had uttered that word, but it was something, and Eli was more sure than ever that he wanted a relationship with Parker. The longer he stayed in Moonlight Falls, the more he could see himself living here. Even if Parker wasn't interested, Eli was tempted to look into what kind of career he could build here.

While that was all exciting, and he had a few ideas about the work he could do, it wasn't important tonight. His mind was focused on kissing and other things.

Eli knocked on Parker's door, wondering what Parker would do if he just flung himself into his arms.

Parker's eyes swept over Eli as he opened the door, and Eli almost pounced. "You're killing me with that look."

Eli blinked. "What look?"

"Ha." Parker grabbed him by the hand and pulled him inside. "Like you don't know."

Eli was going to say he really didn't, but Parker hadn't let go of his hand. He let himself be led all the way to the kitchen, just enjoying the heat of Parker's palm against his.

"Want a drink?" Parker asked.

"Sure." Eli tried not to regret his choice when it meant Parker had to let go of him.

Parker opened two beers and handed one to Eli. "I thought maybe we could play pool, then have dinner later."

"Pool?" Eli couldn't stifle his groan. "You better not say I need practice again."

"No, I just had fun playing with you last time." Parker flashed a dazzling smile before sipping his drink.

Eli blushed.

Parker only smiled wider. "Come on."

They started a game, and this time, there was no doubt Parker was flirting. He was smiling and teasing and couldn't keep his hands off Eli, who turned to putty almost instantly. They kept missing their shots, which only made things more fun.

When Eli finally got a ball in, Parker kissed him.

He backed Eli into the pool table, his hands cradling Eli's face. Parker kissed Eli like he wasn't holding anything back, his tongue taking over Eli's mouth. It stole Eli's breath and made his mind go blank. All he could focus on was everywhere they touched.

Eli perched on the table, legs spread, and pulled Parker in so their bodies were flush. He gripped Parker's broad shoulders and kissed him back like his life depended on it.

"I've never wanted to kiss someone so much," Parker murmured into Eli's mouth.

Eli only managed a groan in response. Part of him still couldn't believe Parker was into him. The other part of him just wanted to see Parker without his shirt.

Eli pulled back and briefly dipped a hand under Parker's T-shirt, skimming his abs. He let his hands roam, mapping Parker's chest, then back, feeling him flex. "You feel so good," he breathed.

Parker leaned in close until his hard cock pressed against Eli's inner thigh. "So do you."

Eli wrapped his arms around Parker's neck and drank in the lusty expression on Parker's face. He liked seeing Parker's full lips reddened from kissing him. It made him ache.

Parker's eyes flashed mischievously. "There's that look again." Before Eli could respond, Parker picked him up in one fluid motion, grip firm on his ass.

Eli gasped and wrapped his legs around Parker's waist. He clung to Parker's shoulders. How was this the most thrilling thing that had ever happened to him? He'd never have thought being carried would be a turn-on.

"I got you," Parker murmured. He took Eli out of the pool room and down the hall to his bedroom. "This okay?" Parker asked as they entered the room.

"Yeah," Eli breathed, looking down at Parker for once. "You can carry me anywhere you damn well please."

Parker huffed a laugh before tossing Eli down on his bed. "Good to know."

Eli lay back and spread his legs, allowing Parker to settle between them. Excitement coursed through Eli as Parker's weight came down on him. They were in bed together.

Parker looked as thrilled as Eli. He threaded his fingers through the hair at the back of Parker's head, holding on and letting the sensation of being pressed together fill his whole world.

Parker traced the line of Eli's jaw with his finger. "So you know, I got tested last month, and I'm negative."

Eli blinked, his heart rate picking up. Right. This was a chat they needed to have. "My last STI test was ages ago, but I, um, haven't been with anyone since. So I'm negative too."

"Sounds like we're all clear." Parker smiled. Eli nodded. "We can go back to kissing now."

That sounded good to Eli. Only, he was more nervous now

than he'd been a second ago. "I haven't been with a man before," he whispered, needing to make it clear.

"That's okay." Parker laid a soft kiss on his lips. "I want you because I like you, Eli, not because I have any expectations of what we'll do in bed together. Being with a new partner is about learning what the other person likes. It's not a performance or a test. We're doing this together."

"You're right." A wave of lust swept over Eli, pushing his nervousness to the back of his mind. Parker being his understanding, caring self, turned him on. He felt safe, comfortable, and genuinely like he couldn't get this wrong. "I'm glad it's you I get to do this with for the first time."

"Me too." Parker kissed him, letting his lips linger. "We don't have to do more than kiss. I'm enjoying getting to know this side of you. There's no rush for anything more."

Eli pulled Parker close, a pleasurable fluttering gripping his chest. "Okay."

Their lips met, and Eli got lost in the feeling of tongues tangling and hands exploring. He rocked his hips under Parker, and Parker moved with him, groaning into his mouth.

This time wasn't as overwhelming as when they'd kissed on the couch. Eli enjoyed every little thing about being close to Parker. His smell. The soft, hungry noises he made. His rough palm against his cheek.

True to his word, Parker didn't push them to do more than kiss. Eli liked knowing they could have done nothing else and Parker wouldn't have minded, but it wasn't enough for Eli. He needed more. Needed all of Parker. He'd waited so long to be in his arms, longer than the past month, longer than he'd known.

"Want to take off our clothes?" Eli asked when he thought the lack of skin-to-skin would kill him.

"Fuck yeah." Parker sat up, grinning and pulling off his shirt.

Eli stared. The man was beautiful. His muscles were defined, his chest dusted with short, coarse hair. Eli ran a hand over his pecs. Parker's eyes fell closed and his lips parted. Eli was drunk off that look of bliss alone. He swept the pad of his thumb over Parker's nipple, and Parker sucked in a breath.

Eli did it again. "You like that?"

"Yes." Parker smoldered down at him. "Feel free to pinch or bite my nipples if you're into it."

Fuck, this was hot. Eli was blown away by how deep his desire for Parker went. He wasn't thinking about it being his first time with a man anymore. He was wrapped up in Parker's reactions and all the possibilities between them, all the new things they could learn about each other, even after so many years. Eli wanted to make Parker feel good. He wanted to discover every little thing he liked.

Eli pinched Parker's nipple and was rewarded with a moan. His cock ached. He sat up and licked Parker where he'd pinched him, savoring the taste of his skin. Eli sucked and flicked his tongue against Parker's hard nipple as he reached for Parker's pants, popping the button.

"Oh fuck, Eli." Parker groaned, cupping the back of Eli's head, holding him close.

They only separated to get their pants and Eli's shirt off. When they were down to their boxer briefs, Parker raked his gaze over Eli. His attention lingered on Eli's chest, then on the bulge between his legs. The heat in Parker's eyes was addictive, and before he could think better of it, Eli pulled his underwear away, letting his dick spring free.

"Gorgeous," Parker rumbled.

Eli tingled all over. He pulled Parker back down on top of him, and his brain short-circuited. He'd never been this hyper-aware of touch during sex. Their bodies pressed so close shattered Eli's world for what felt like the millionth time in the last few weeks. Parker and him together was everything.

As they kissed, Eli worked Parker's boxer briefs down. The moment their dicks brushed with nothing separating them, Eli made an obscene sound. Fuck, he was going to come just knowing they were completely naked together.

"You feel so good, Eli," Parker whispered in his ear as they moved. "I love feeling you against me. Love the way you can't hold back. You're so hot, baby. I can't stand it."

"Fuck." Eli stopped moving and took a second to breathe. "Parker, I've never felt anything like this."

Parker smiled at him, a lust-drunk glint in his eye. "Do you want to get off like this? I could jerk us both together." He wrapped a big hand around their cocks to demonstrate.

Eli whimpered. The sight of their two dripping tips pushed together, protruding from Parker's hand, was the most erotic thing Eli had ever seen. He wouldn't last more than a stroke or two if Parker did what he'd suggested.

"Can I suck you off?" Eli panted, desperate not to come yet.

"*God yes.*" Parker let go of them and leaned down to kiss him. "Love your mouth on me."

Eli loved his mouth on Parker too. He loved the reactions he got from playing with his nipples, so he figured his mouth on Parker's dick would be even better.

Parker climbed off him and lay back on the pillows. He looked like a god, chiseled and tanned, face flushed from fooling around. Eli could have watched him for an eternity.

He settled between Parker's legs and wrapped his hand around Parker's flushed erection. He stroked it, watching Parker's hooded gaze track the movement. Someone else's cock felt so different from his own. Parker was thicker than he was, longer too, but it was more than that. Knowing he was touching Parker made his chest warm and his insides squirm with pleasure.

Eli needed to taste him. He leaned down and swiped his tongue over Parker's tip, lapping up the precum beading at his slit. Eli groaned at the taste as Parker let out a satisfied *oomph*. He explored with his tongue, from Parker's balls, up his shaft, and back down again.

"That feels amazing, Eli," Parker moaned, his hand resting lightly on Eli's head.

Eli appreciated the praise. He knew this wouldn't be the most skilled blowjob Parker had ever received, but that didn't matter. This was about the two of them together and showing Parker how much he liked him.

Eli took Parker's cock into his mouth and sucked on his tip. The stretch of his lips felt obscene and totally exciting. He bobbed his head experimentally, letting his tongue do some more exploring.

Parker ran a hand through Eli's hair. "Yeah, like that."

Eli did it again before taking Parker a little deeper. He groaned as he sucked, the sensation of Parker filling his mouth better than he'd imagined. He couldn't take Parker all the way down, at least not without more practice, but he wanted to be filled as much as possible. He wanted Parker to come in his mouth.

He worked Parker more vigorously, smiling when Parker gave a tiny thrust of his hips. Eli looked up, cock still in his mouth, and caught Parker's eye. He looked wrecked, maybe even desperate. Eli bobbed his head, keeping his gaze on Parker as best he could. He didn't want to miss any of this.

"You're gorgeous with my dick in your mouth." Parker's voice was rough. His hips twitched again. "Fuck, keep doing that, and I'm gonna come."

Eli sucked as enthusiastically as he could. Soon, Parker moaned one last warning, his hands tugging gently on Eli's hair. Eli didn't pull off, and Parker came in his mouth. The sensation was a bit startling, even though Eli was expecting it, but his shock only turned him on. He liked being overwhelmed by Parker. Eli kept sucking, drinking Parker down, and basked in the feel of Parker's cock jerking against his tongue.

He pulled off and wiped his mouth. His whole body felt hot, aching with longing. Fuck, he couldn't wait to do that again.

"Come here." Parker tugged Eli up the bed until he was on the big man's lap. "That was amazing."

"Yeah?" Eli smiled, sure his cheeks were as red as humanly possible.

"Yeah." Parker leaned in and kissed him, sweeping his tongue over Eli's. "Now it's your turn if you want?"

Eli went momentarily lightheaded. "Yes, I'd love that."

Parker gave him a devilish grin. He didn't waste any time getting between Eli's legs, but he didn't go right for his cock. Parker kissed Eli's belly button before moving to his hips and thighs. He nuzzled his nose against Eli's groin and let out a rumbling groan.

Eli was leaking precum and knew there was no way he'd last. The sight of Parker kneeling before him was a literal dream.

Parker made eye contact as he took Eli into his mouth. Eli couldn't stop the sound he made, not that there was any reason to. He wanted Parker to know how good he was making him feel. Parker's mouth was hot and tight as he sucked, and he did this magic thing with his tongue. Eli ran his hands through Parker's hair, and in no time at all, his orgasm was building.

"Parker," he whined in warning. "Gonna make me come."

Parker only took him deeper, sliding down Eli's shaft until his nose met the hair framing his cock. With a shout, Eli came down his throat, the image of Parker swallowing cemented in his mind forever.

Eli flopped back onto the pillows, pulling Parker up to join him. "I want to do that every day."

Parker chuckled, throwing an arm over Eli. "I don't see any reason why we can't."

# CHAPTER TWELVE

They had dinner much later. Eli opted to stay the night at Parker's—as if he'd do anything else once the man had asked.

Sleeping over came with the benefit of not needing to deal with shades on the way to his car, but the downside of having to text James. His brother hadn't said anything when Eli mentioned he was hanging out with Parker, but there was no way James wouldn't know what was going on now that Eli was spending the night.

But that was fine. Eli wasn't worried about James finding out he was starting something with his best friend. Eli was more confident about where he and Parker stood now, and if anything, it would probably make James happy to see Eli with Parker. It'd probably give him hope Eli would stay in Moonlight Falls.

For the first time, thinking about James's desire to have him around more didn't fill Eli with guilt. Not seeing James enough was one of the things he hated about living so far away.

THE NEXT FEW weeks were the happiest of Eli's life. His research went well, he enjoyed working at the diner, and the time he spent with Parker blew his mind.

It wasn't just sex making him feel that way. One Wednesday afternoon, Parker took Eli hiking. They chose a trail west of town, so Eli hadn't brought any of his research equipment. Which was fine with him. He would much rather spend time with Parker, not working, not researching, just being together.

The trail Parker suggested didn't have a lot of elevation change and made for easy walking, with a wide path winding through the trees. Parker grabbed Eli's hand as they started and didn't let go. Holding hands was so simple, yet Eli's heart just about exploded. He leaned into Parker, their shoulders touching, and squeezed their palms together.

"Look." Parker pointed through the trees. Two deer stood barely a hundred feet away. Parker and Eli froze, watching. Parker leaned in to whisper in Eli's ear, "They're so cute."

Eli smiled. Parker was adorable.

When the deer moved on, Parker let out a soft sigh like he'd wanted to watch the animals longer. "Come on, there's a good picnic spot not far away." He pulled Eli along, smiling like he was having the best day ever.

As they walked along, Parker commented on the surrounding plants. "Did you know there's a wildlife club in town now?"

"Really?"

"Don't sound so surprised." Parker bumped Eli's shoulder playfully. "Stuff changes around here. It's not all exactly the same as when you left."

Eli knew Parker was right. In the past, the comment might have annoyed him. Now, it didn't bother him at all. Parker wasn't hassling him, and Eli wasn't trying so hard to dislike Moonlight Falls. The club sounded cool. "Did you join?"

"Of course. I had to keep my plant knowledge up to date after you stopped taking tree classes."

Eli laughed. "I never took a tree class, but I wish I had. Sounds awesome."

Parker talked about some of the trips the club took and a summer program they were putting together for local kids. It sounded like Parker loved it, and it seemed like he'd gotten into it all because of Eli and his apparently infections enthusiasm for nature facts. Which was wild. Eli was an important part of Parker's life and had been for a while.

Eli liked everything about that. It made it seem like there were endless ways for them to fit their lives together. "How often does the club meet?"

Parker stopped at a wooden picnic table nestled off the path. "Once a month, but we organize walks and things more often than that."

"Can I come with you next time?"

"Of course." Parker beamed, cupping Eli's face in his hands. "You'll love it."

Eli had no doubt he would, and he'd enjoy it even more, having it be something he and Parker did together.

Parker pulled off his backpack and set it on the table. He produced a thermos, and upon opening it, Eli was greeted with the sweet smell of coffee, prepared with cream and sugar, just how he liked it.

Parker handed Eli a cashew nut granola bar. "I've got fruit salad and sandwiches too."

The granola bar was the one Eli always chose out of the mixed pack. "Yum. I love this one." He smiled, and Parker's cheeks flushed.

Parker handed Eli a Tupperware container of pears, apples, pomegranate seeds, and chopped walnuts. The sandwiches were cucumber and turkey. This wasn't just any fruit salad and sandwiches. They were Eli's personal favorites.

Eli got choked up, emotion stealing his breath. All this had been prepared just for him. Maybe that was simple, and Eli was easy to please, but it felt meaningful. "Thank you, Parker. This is perfect."

Parker slung an arm around him and kissed the top of his head. "Glad you like it, gorgeous. I've had this afternoon in mind for a while."

Eli's heart swelled. This thing with Parker might be new, but it felt like his whole life had led him to this perfect day, sitting in the arms of a man who knew him better than anyone.

THE REST of the week flew by. They still hadn't defined what they were, but Eli knew what he wanted. There was no point waiting to bring it up. He was sure he wanted to be with Parker. He'd never clicked so well with another person and needed to see what the two of them could build together.

He arrived at Parker's house for another overnight and knocked on the door. As soon as it opened, Parker pulled him into a deep kiss. Eli had planned to talk to Parker first, but the next thing he knew, they were in Parker's bedroom, and he wasn't complaining.

Eli's body burned for Parker. Every sweet thing Parker did only made Eli's desire grow. There was still an exciting newness to being with Parker and the way their bodies felt together, but it was the familiarity between them that really made Eli's heart race.

They stripped each other naked and fell onto the bed. Parker's body caged Eli in, pressing him into the mattress and filling his whole world.

"Parker." Eli cupped his face, breaking their kiss.

Parker gazed down at him. "Yes, gorgeous?"

"I just—I like you so much."

Parker's look turned sweet as he smiled. "I like you too, Eli. I don't think I'll ever get enough of you."

"Same." Eli took a heaving breath. "But we don't have to get enough of each other. I want to be with you. I want to date you, tell everyone we're a couple, and call you my boyfriend."

"I'd love that," Parker whispered. "I'd love to be your boyfriend."

Eli pulled Parker's lips back to his and kissed him. They were nothing but hands on sweaty skin, hard cocks grinding together, and Eli was so happy. He felt like he had everything, but a greedy part wanted more.

Eli arched his back, his breath heaving. "Fuck me, Parker. Please."

Parker stilled on top of him, hunger in his eyes. "You sure, gorgeous?"

Eli nodded emphatically, and Parker seemed to soak up his enthusiasm. He kissed Eli hard on the mouth until Eli was squirming.

Parker moved his lips down Eli's body, kissing him hungrily. He knelt between Eli's legs, and Eli spread himself wide. Parker ran his big hands along Eli's inner thighs like he was touching something precious. He took his time caressing Eli, giving attention to his balls and taint.

Eli squirmed. "Please."

The pad of Parker's thumb brushed his hole. "You sure you want this?"

"Yes." Eli's whole body quivered. "Every time I finger myself, I think about you fucking me."

"*Shit.*" Parker closed his eyes like he needed a second to collect himself. He squeezed his cock and fixed Eli with a hooded gaze. "I need to see that sometime."

Eli bit his lip. "Yeah, I'd love you watching me." He wanted to see Parker get himself off too.

"But not now." Parker reached for his bedside table, retrieving lube and a condom.

Eli's heart pounded. He wanted this badly but couldn't deny the tinge of anxiety beneath his arousal. He'd never had anything as big as Parker inside him. No one else had even fingered him. It had always been something he'd done alone.

Parker's slick finger massaged Eli's puckered flesh. Eli whined needily, even as his muscles tensed. Parker stroked his hip soothingly with his other hand. "Relax for me. I've got you."

Eli tried to relax. It felt amazing. Having someone else's finger down there was so different.

Parker began stroking Eli's cock as his other hand worked between his legs, and Eli felt himself unwind. When Parker finally pressed his finger in, Eli moaned in relief, not only relaxed but desperate to be touched at his core.

Parker finger-fucked him slowly, in and out, until he was buried deep. Then he crooked his finger, stroking over Eli's prostate.

Eli moaned, back arched, as pleasure coursed through him.

"That's it, gorgeous," Parker murmured as he did it again.

Eli writhed and pressed into Parker's touch. Firm fingers slowly opened him up, and when Parker got to adding a third, Eli had never felt so full.

"More," he begged.

Parker withdrew and smiled at Eli's whimper. He rolled on a condom and lubed up but sat up against the headboard next to Eli. "You want to be on top?"

"Like ride your cock?" Eli asked, dazed.

"Yeah." Parker pulled Eli up next to him. "It's a good position for your first time. You set the pace."

Eli blushed. Which was silly, given Parker had just been knuckle-deep inside him. "Okay."

He straddled Parker's lap, his hands braced on Parker's shoulders. They shared a look. Parker's expression seemed bright with excitement and wonder. It floored Eli. He crashed their mouths together, trying to show Parker how much this meant to him.

Eli reached back and took hold of Parker's cock. He broke the kiss and looked down at his erection painting Parker's abs with precum. He lined Parker up with his hole. At the feeling of Parker's blunt head against his pucker, Eli's eyes snapped back to Parker's.

Parker gripped his hips, not putting any pressure on Eli to sink down, just holding him. "You're so fucking sexy right now, Eli."

Eli bit his lip. Parker was the hottest man he'd ever known, and he was laid out beneath Eli, ready and waiting. How mind-blowing was that? "So are you, Parker."

Eli pressed down. The head of Parker's cock pushed past his tight ring of muscle, and Parker groaned, his hands tightening on Eli's hips. Eli gasped. A dick was so much bigger than fingers. The stretch burned, so he waited, holding just the tip inside him. It wasn't bad, not painful in a way he couldn't get past, just a lot.

Parker pressed their noses together as Eli took a second to adjust. "Take your time. You feel amazing."

The only response Eli could manage was a whimper. He sank a little farther, then lifted himself back up. He wrapped his arms tight around Parker's neck, panting into his mouth, too overwhelmed to coordinate kissing. Parker rubbed his thighs, hands circling around to Eli's ass, then back to his hips.

As the initial discomfort faded, Eli took Parker slowly, inch by inch.

"So good," Parker moaned, his grip tightening, thumbs tracing circles over Eli's skin. "You're being so good for me, Eli. Look at you—you're perfect."

Eli couldn't find words, only moans and whimpers. He felt too full, so consumed by what they were doing, and he loved it. When he was fully seated, he let his eyes flutter closed, just feeling it. Feeling Parker.

"How're you doing, gorgeous?" Parker asked as he caressed Eli's hips.

"Amazing." Eli held Parker close. "Your cock feels so good."

Parker wrapped his hand around Eli's half-hard dick and stroked. Soon, he was fully erect again, the distraction of adjusting to being penetrated replaced with nothing but a need for more.

Eli gave an experimental roll of his hips, and they both groaned. Parker was so deep inside him.

Eli ground himself onto Parker, finding a rhythm that sent pleasure rolling through him. He took Parker's mouth in a messy kiss, and Parker's tongue tangled with his.

Parker met Eli's thrusts with his own, still letting him set the pace, but each snap of Parker's hips rocked Eli's world. Before long, he was bouncing on Parker's dick, his head fallen back, crying out each time he came back down.

Eli made himself focus through his lust haze. He needed to see Parker as well as feel him. Parker seemed mesmerized, his gaze locked on Eli, clearly loving this as much as Eli.

"I'm close," Eli moaned, fucking Parker harder.

Parker matched his intensity, thrusting deep as he jerked Eli off with a tight fist. "Come for me, gorgeous."

That was it for Eli. Cum spilled over Parker's abs as Eli clenched around his cock. He dug his nails into Parker's shoulders as he rode out his orgasm, moaning, "Fuck, fuck, fuck."

Parker thrust into Eli, and just as Eli's orgasm crested, Parker gave a shout, and Eli felt him jolt deep inside him. He pulled Parker impossibly closer as Parker came in jerks, face buried in Eli's neck.

Parker pulled back, panting, a dopey, somewhat smug grin on his face. Eli loved it. Their mouths met in a breathless kiss.

Eli snuggled into Parker. He'd never felt so close to another person. Parker's hand came to rest on the small of his back, and he felt like he was home. Safe. He never wanted to be anywhere else.

After a while, they disentangled themselves and cleaned up, then crawled back into bed. Eli rested his head on Parker's chest and listened to his heartbeat.

Parker's hand found its way into Eli's hair. "How was it?"

Eli huffed a laugh. "Mind-blowing. Something I expect to do again soon."

Parker chucked. "You won't get an argument from me."

"You should bend me over the pool table next time," Eli said without hesitation.

"What?" Parker sounded totally shocked, which pleased Eli to no end.

"It's just something I've been thinking about since we played at the barbecue."

"Huh." Parker trailed his fingers down Eli's spine. "Wish I'd known."

"I'd have died of embarrassment if you'd figured out what I was thinking that day." Eli turned his head to look up at Parker. "I was only just coming to terms with having a crush on you. I liked you before I knew what my feelings meant. That's how drawn to you I am. Not even believing I was straight could stand in the way."

A soft, vulnerable look passed over Parker's face. "Yeah?"

"Yeah." Eli hugged him tight. "I've never felt so comfortable being myself with someone as I do with you. I know I'm having a lot of firsts with you, but what I'm feeling isn't just about fully embracing my sexuality. It's about you. I don't think anything will ever feel as right as the two of us together. The way I want you goes so deep. I think it's always been part of me. I think I'm falling for you, Parker. Like really falling for you."

Parker squeezed him close and dropped a kiss on his forehead. "I've been falling for you for a long time, Eli. You've been dazzling me for years with how clever you are. You're the most fascinating person I know. I never stood a chance. Your smile stops me in my tracks. I love being around you—you make my whole world feel brighter than should be possible—it makes me never want to give you up."

"You won't ever have to."

Parker cupped his face. "Good. I wouldn't know how, now that I've got you." Parker hesitated, fingers tracing Eli's cheek. "I never thought I'd get to spend this much time with you. Never thought you'd stick around. I've held back the last couple of years —even though I liked you more and more each time I saw you— because I didn't want to ruin what we had. You're so important to James. I couldn't risk things getting awkward between us, and I didn't want to become another reason you avoided Moonlight Falls."

Eli's heart pinched. He'd had no idea. Parker had liked him for years and had been waiting for him to give them a chance.

"I'd have been happy being your friend, Eli. But this is so much better."

Eli crawled up Parker's chest and kissed him. *So much better* didn't even cover it.

# CHAPTER THIRTEEN

THE NEXT DAY passed in a haze. Eli managed to get some of his research done, but barely. His thoughts were on nothing but Parker.

Eli wanted to tell everyone. But he hadn't yet. He couldn't tell anyone that he and Parker were official until he told his brother, and he'd missed James that morning before he'd left for the electrical shop. Eli wouldn't see James until late that evening when he got off from the dinner shift at the diner.

Waiting to tell James was killing him. His shift seemed to inch by. Business was steady but not busy enough to keep him from constantly checking the clock.

Eli thought Kaylin suspected something was going on between him and Parker. She'd started making comments about how lovely the two of them were whenever she caught them talking.

Once they'd finished closing down, Eli rushed out the door, calling goodbye to the others as he went. Parker knew Eli was itching to tell James about their relationship, and his amused chuckle followed Eli out the door.

Eli unlocked his car. A strange woosh behind him made him

pause. Something sharp clamped down on his shoulders before he could process the sound further. Eli was yanked backward. He stumbled, only just catching himself from falling.

Shadows wrapped around his legs.

Eli twisted, but the shade behind him moved, releasing his shoulders. Damn it. Eli's keys, along with his light, were dangling out of reach in the driver's door. He lunged for them.

The shade surrounded him in shadow. Soon, Eli couldn't see, completely enveloped in dense, inky blackness. He yelled, hoping to draw attention from the people inside the diner. This wasn't normal. Shades didn't use their shadow magic like this. He hadn't even realized it was among their powers.

Then, the darkness was gone. The shade loomed before him. It was huge, it's body more solid and imposing than waspy. It hissed, baring its teeth, and pounced.

Eli yelled again, throwing his hands up to protect himself from the sharp teeth coming toward him. The shade bit down, cutting through his denim jacket and piercing his skin. The thing latched on and didn't let go. Eli struggled, but the shade's arms wrapped around his body, tightening steadily until he gasped for breath.

Peripherally, Eli noticed a commotion at the diner's back door. Light flared, bright as day. A ball of white hot energy hit the shade and light burst from within it. The shade exploded into whisps of black smoke and was gone.

"Eli!" Parker shouted. In a blink, he was at Eli's side, reaching for his arm.

"It bit me," Eli said in disbelief.

"Let me see." Parker carefully took Eli's jacket off, exposing his bloody arm.

"Should I call someone?" Kaylin asked from behind Parker.

Parker inspected the wound thoroughly. "I think we're okay. It doesn't look deep. Good thing you were wearing denim and not just a hoodie. I don't think you'll need stitches."

"Eli?" Kaylin looked to him for confirmation. "Are you okay?"

"Yeah, it's all right, Kaylin." Eli's voice shook, but he was safe with Parker.

"I've got a first aid kit in my car." Parker led Eli over. He grabbed a large gauze bandage and pressed it over the wound. "Let's get you home so we can clean this."

Eli nodded and got in Parker's car. After double checking they didn't need anything, Kaylin got in her own vehicle and drove off.

It only took a few minutes to get Eli home. Inside, he led Parker to the downstairs bathroom across from his bedroom.

He shivered. "It attacked me out of nowhere," he tried to explain, still in disbelief. "It wasn't just messing around. It was like it wanted to hurt me from the start. If you hadn't gotten there—" His voice trailed off.

"I don't like the sound of that." Parker directed Eli to the sink to wash his arm. "But you're safe now. It's okay. The teeth didn't get a chance to tear your skin, only puncture it."

Eli nodded. The water stung. He heard James call out from upstairs. Parker called back, and soon, his brother was outside the bathroom.

"Oh my god, Eli!" James rushed up to him, grabbing his shoulder. "What happened?"

Eli explained again. The fear on his brother's face nearly killed him. He hated causing James worry.

"It attacked," Parker said plainly. "If I hadn't banished it, it didn't look like it would stop at one bite. I've never seen a shade take hold of someone like that. It was like it wanted to devour him."

James blanched, his face pale.

Eli felt a surge of residual fear. "Something's not right," he managed to say. "The shades have seemed different ever since I got here. They never used to seek out human contact. Never got aggressive outside of self-defense."

"They're a bit more interactive now than they used to be, but *not* like this." James crossed his arms and stared at a random spot on the wall, thinking. "We'll have to report what happened and see what we can do to keep people safe. If something is changing, then there's the chance this could happen again."

Eli dried his arm and pressed a clean bandage to it. James nudged him and handed him some antiseptic cream. Once that was applied, Parker wrapped the bandage in gauze to secure it.

Eli looked up from the wound. "Could the shades have been following me specifically?"

James and Parker looked at him with twin furrows in their brows, both men frowning.

"I know it sounds ridiculous," Eli admitted. "But it was a thought I had after one followed me home from Parker's a couple of weeks ago."

"It's unlikely," Parker said carefully. "We should ask around and see if other people have been dealing with more aggressive shades. If we discover that no one but you has noticed anything out of the ordinary, then it's possible they were targeting you."

"We'll figure this out." James squeezed Eli's shoulder.

Parker pulled out his phone and shot off a text. To whom, Eli wasn't sure.

"Come on." James led the way out of the cramped bathroom. "Let's go sit down."

They settled in the living room. Eli instinctively cuddled against Parker on the couch. He felt secure with the big man's arm around him and his heartbeat under his ear. Eli breathed a sigh of relief, then looked up to find James staring at them.

His brother's gaze quickly flicked away.

"I meant to talk to you when I got home tonight, James." Eli straightened as his brother's attention returned to him. "Parker and I are dating. And um, yeah." He gestured between himself and his boyfriend unnecessarily.

James smiled, some of the worry lines leaving his face. "I figured something was going on."

"Well, it's official." Eli couldn't hide his smile.

Parker's arm tightened around him and the two friends exchanged a look. "You should give this romance thing a chance, James. Eli just might be the best thing that's ever happened to me."

James huffed and shook his head. "I'm glad for you—both of you—but I'm good."

Eli agreed with Parker, but he'd learned to stop asking about James's dating life a long time ago.

Parker's phone buzzed and he quickly read the incoming text. "The mayor says there have been several reports of unusual shade activity in the last month. Nothing this violent, but tending toward aggressive. She's concerned about what just happened to Eli. She wants to meet in the morning."

James nodded.

"Should I come?" Eli looked between them.

"If you want." James eyed him cautiously. "You can explain to Eleanor what happened, but you don't have to. Parker and I can pass it on."

"But she's going to ask you guys to help her with the problem, right? If it's not just me, and shades are getting aggressive in general, the town has to do something." Eli was relieved he hadn't been the only one targeted, even if he'd been the only one bitten. He'd known thinking shades were stalking him specifically was out there, even for Moonlight Falls, but still, having the suspicion disproven was reassuring.

"Yeah, she'll probably ask us to help," Parker agreed. "I do a lot of protective spells for the town, and James and Hazel cover anything handy."

Eli knew Parker and his brother were pretty involved in the inner workings of Moonlight Falls. He felt he better understood their desire to do that now. Before, he'd dismissed it as unwarranted loyalty due to their belief that the town called to them, but they just wanted to give back to the community and look after the people here. Parker took care of people. It was a big part of who he was. Same with James.

And maybe Eli didn't have to feel so guilty about James looking after him when he was younger. James probably didn't resent it, and Eli wouldn't be surprised to find James offering to look after anyone he cared about.

"I want to help if I can," Eli insisted.

"You're going to get involved in town affairs?" James's eyebrows traveled up his forehead. "Voluntarily?"

Eli crossed his arms, feeling Parker's body shake against him in silent laughter. "Yes, I am."

"That's great." James broke into a smile, his shock lingering in his widened eyes.

They were quiet for a moment. Eli closed his eyes and leaned into Parker.

"You sure you're all right, Eli?" his brother asked.

Eli opened his eyes. "Yeah, just kind of exhausted all the sudden."

"You should rest." James stood. He nodded to Parker. "I'll see you two in the morning." With that, he retreated upstairs.

Eli pulled Parker into his bedroom. "Thanks for looking after me."

Parker wrapped him in a hug. "Of course. I'll always take care of you. Just like I know you'll take care of me."

Eli burrowed his face into Parker's chest. "You're right, I will."

"Tonight isn't putting you off Moonlight Falls?" There was hesitation in Parker's voice. "This shade attack isn't making you want to get the hell out of here as soon as possible?"

Eli pulled back to stare up at Parker. He seemed vulnerable and unsure in a way Eli had never seen before. "No," Eli said without doubt. "I'm done letting bad accidents rule my life. This place is so much more than painful memories or bloodthirsty shades. I feel like now that I've let go of that, I can be happy here in a way that I can't anywhere else. It's home."

Parker brushed a lock of hair off Eli's forehead. "I know what you mean. Moonlight Falls calls us home. But it feels more like home with you here than ever before."

Eli's chest tightened. "I feel at home with you too, Parker." He squeezed him until he thought he would burst with all the feelings he had for this man. He'd never thought things could be this good, especially here. But he was glad to be wrong.

# CHAPTER FOURTEEN

That Sunday, they all gathered at Parker's, this time for the chef's special casserole rather than a barbecue since it was raining. They were all in the kitchen, Hazel leaning against the counter next to James.

She turned her attention to Eli. "How's your research going?"

Eli closed the fridge with a bump of his hip, two beers in hand. He gave one to Parker. "Good. I've got my recording box in a new location, and I've started doing some mapping through the neighborhoods."

Parker popped the cap off his beer, handed it back to Eli, and took the other for himself. "We're going to hit the trails soon too."

Hazel looked momentarily confused. "For the study?"

"Yeah." Parker opened the other beer. "Eli needs to map the vein north of town."

"Oh." Hazel nodded and took a slow sip of her drink like something didn't add up.

Eli gave James a look. "You didn't tell Hazel that Parker and I are together, did you?"

"No." James's brow crinkled. "Was I supposed to?"

Eli huffed. "Well, it's not a secret."

"Yeah, James." Hazel shoved his shoulder in a friendly-yet-annoyed fashion. "Could have told me."

James grunted, a sure sign he was ignoring everything they were saying.

Eli laughed at his brother and leaned against Parker. "I've actually got more news for you all. Beyond my dating life."

Parker tipped Eli's shin up so their eyes met. "You do?"

Eli beamed up at him. "Not new news to you. But kind of?"

Parker's eyes narrowed as he smiled. "Ooo…kay. I have no idea what you're talking about."

Eli was making a big deal of this, but it felt justified. He took a breath and announced, "I want to move back here after I'm done with my degree."

Hazel choked on her beer. James thumped her on the back, a look of tentative joy on his face.

"I've been thinking," Eli went on. "I want to study the magic here. More than I'm doing just for my thesis. I mean, I'm only looking at one aspect of the vein. There's so much more to investigate."

James set his drink aside like he didn't want it distracting him. "And you can do that?"

Eli shrugged, but his smile didn't dim. "It's not guaranteed. I'd need to get a job at a university or research institute after I graduate and apply for a study grant. But I think there's enough unique magic around Moonlight Falls that I'll be able to find someone to fund research up here."

James crossed his arms. "What about your life in LA?"

It was like he needed to cover all the bases before he'd believe this might actually happen. Eli got where James was coming from. Still, he suppressed a sigh. He didn't like having to admit this.

"I'm not going to miss LA. I already don't. I actually like living somewhere small and quiet, and I'd miss everyone here if I left way more than I've missed the people I know down south. I'm not that close to anyone. It's nothing like this." He gestured at everyone in the kitchen.

Eli would lose a lot if he left Moonlight Falls, while he only felt like he was gaining good things by leaving LA. It wasn't that he didn't have friends, but he didn't have anyone he was genuinely attached to. He had lots of study partners and roommates but not a best friend or anyone who came close. Eli had always been more of a relationship person, opening up to his girlfriends but not so much with anyone else. As a result, he didn't have anyone worth moving back to LA for.

And here in Moonlight Falls, he had everyone. Eli wanted to make up for lost time with James. He wanted to be there for his brother now that he was older. Eli wanted James to know they could look after each other. Neither of them were alone, even if they were the last people left in their family.

And, of course, there was Parker, whom Eli could see a whole future with. Parker had always been there, always paid attention and been interested in Eli's life, always wanted to include him. Parker cared deeply, and not just because he was James's brother. Parker had liked Eli in his own right as a friend and then, over the past couple of years, as something more. Eli would move home for that, even if there was nothing else.

But there was. Eli had Hazel and the potential to get to know Sam again. He had a whole damn town that was interested in his research, itching to help him with it, and wanting to see him succeed.

Eli also suspected that allowing himself to love this place would bring him closer to everyone he'd lost. His parents and grandparents had loved Moonlight Falls as much as Parker did. It could be a way to connect with them, even if they weren't here.

"We'd miss you if you left again," Hazel said, surprisingly genuine, before adding, "Plus, I'm not going to talk you out of it when you're just one more person to beat at pool."

Eli laughed.

James gave Hazel an exasperated look, then enveloped Eli in a hug. "I'm so happy," he whispered in Eli's ear.

"Me too," Eli whispered back.

Deciding to stay in Moonlight Falls gave him a settled feeling he hadn't known he'd longed for. Like he'd been restless or searching for something over the past five years and had finally found it. Maybe it was part of the town's magic. Maybe it was knowing he was surrounded by people who loved him. Either way, this place was home.

The End

Looking for more from Moonlight Falls? James and Sebastian's story starts with *The Seduction of James Gray.*

Need more of Eli and Parker? Don't miss *Playing Pool,* a steamy bonus scene exclusive to my newsletter subscribers. Join now and read Parker's point of view as he and Eli have some fun in the pool room.

Want to keep in touch? Join my reader group on Facebook, Colette Rivera's Coven!

# THANK YOU FOR READING THE
# FALL OF ELIJAH GRAY

I hoped you enjoyed Eli and Parker's story.

Reviews are invaluable to authors. Please consider leaving a review for The Fall of Elijah Gray on your favorite review site, or the site where you purchased this book to help others find magical books they'll love.

# THE SEDUCTION OF JAMES GRAY

**Mystery, temptation, and risking it all.**

James Gray lives a life free of complications. Even in Moonlight Falls, a town known for supernatural activity, he stays away from the more sinister magical arts, preferring the simple work of a magical electrician.

Sebastian Storm is a man James hasn't thought about in years until he hears Sebastian inherited the haunted house north of town. Most locals avoid the place. The eccentric Sebastian moves in and requests James's help with electrical problems.

Storm House's shade infestation is the first hitch in the job. The second? Sebastian. He's doing his best to get James into bed. James doesn't want any part of Sebastian's games, no matter how attractive he is, but James begins to wonder if there's more going on at the haunted property than Sebastian will admit.

Uncovering secrets will only bring trouble, but James can't help himself. There's something about Sebastian he can't shake.

What's the worst that could happen if he lets himself be seduced by the mystery as well as the man?

# ACKNOWLEDGMENTS

I would like to thank Abbie Nicole for her excellent editing. I'm constantly in awe of editors and their attention to every detail. I couldn't do it without you.

Many thanks to Sleepy Fox Studio for the gorgeous cover design. Working with designers is always one of my favorite parts of bringing a book to life.

I would also like to thank Laura for talking with me about tropes back when I was organizing ideas for this story. It really helped me bring everything together.

As always, thank you to TK for your love and support. I could not build these magic worlds without you.

And thank you to all my readers. I appreciate every one of you. Your excitement for my stories and kind messages keep me going.

# ABOUT THE AUTHOR

Colette is an author of queer paranormal romance novels. She loves to write couples who take care of each other and show their soft sides when in love. Sugar and spice are key ingredients in all her books. She's an avid PNR reader and loves all things magic. Colette once lived in the US but now calls New Zealand home. As a bisexual she has to resist making all her characters bi. When she succeeds you'll find a variety of representation in her books.

Colette can be found on Instagram @colette_rivera and on Facebook under Colette Rivera Author. She can also be found on her website coletterivera.com where you can sign up to her newsletter for bonus scenes and updates.

# MOONLIGHT FALLS

The Fall of Elijah Gray

The Seduction of James Gray

The Cursed Sebastian Storm

The Heart of Moonlight Falls